Yvonne Boxerman

Unexpected Encounters

Yvonne Boxerman

# Unexpected Encounters

## A Collection of Short Stories

*July 2020,*
*To Andrea,*
*Best wishes,*
*Yvonne*

**Hakodesh Press**

**Imprint**
Any brand names and product names mentioned in this book are subject to trademark, brand or patent protection and are trademarks or registered trademarks of their respective holders. The use of brand names, product names, common names, trade names, product descriptions etc. even without a particular marking in this work is in no way to be construed to mean that such names may be regarded as unrestricted in respect of trademark and brand protection legislation and could thus be used by anyone.

Cover image: www.ingimage.com

Publisher:
Hakodesh Press
is a trademark of
International Book Market Service Ltd., member of OmniScriptum Publishing Group
17 Meldrum Street, Beau Bassin 71504, Mauritius
Printed at: see last page
**ISBN: 978-620-2-45541-1**

*This book is dedicated to my beloved husband, David, and to our*

*wonderful children and their spouses, Aaron and Cindy, Jonathan*

*and Jen, and Miriam and Miles.*

*And to our very special grandchildren, Leah and Norah, Griffin*

*and Wesley, and Sylvie and Isaac.*

# Table of Contents

# Eliahu HaNavi

It was Labor Day, and early that morning before the rest of the household arose, I was busy making challah for the soon-to-be-upon-us High Holidays. Just after the dough was kneaded and covered to rise, I discovered we were out of milk for breakfast. This would be a good time to run to the local liquor store, the only store open in our neighborhood that morning.

Let me take you through the events of the next couple of hours. They had such a profound effect, and are so vividly etched in my memory, that I believe they will stay with me for as long as I live.

I was driving in the far right lane of a six lane thoroughfare near my home when suddenly, close to the liquor store, a very small boy with no one else nearby stepped into the road directly ahead of me. I was far enough away to stop in time, but I knew that a car in the next lane would surely hit him, as my car was blocking any view of this tiny child. Acting on reflex alone, I stopped the car, pulled the hazard signal on, and jumped out leaving the door open so that drivers approaching on my left would have the sense to slow down, if not stop altogether. Then I quickly ran to the front of the car, picked up the child and carried him to the sidewalk. At that very moment, a teenage boy wearing a backwards cap came sauntering down the street. I asked him if he was connected to the child.

"Unh, unh," he said shaking his head.

"Well, please hold him for a minute while I get my car out of the traffic."

Without giving him a chance to refuse, I thrust the child at him. Then I pulled the car into a parking space and came back to retrieve the little fellow.

"Here, take him," said the reluctant babysitter. As soon as the child was safely back with me, the young man started jogging away at an extremely rapid pace!

Now I had a chance to look at the child and assess the situation. A chubby little boy with black hair and sparkling dark eyes, he wore short pants, a blue tee-shirt ripping at the seam, and sneakers without socks. The shoelaces were untied and the shoes very badly worn.

"What's your name, Buddy? Where's Mama?" I asked to no avail. Every question was met by peals of laughter and chubby fingers pointing to planes in the sky and birds in the trees, all of which this little guy found very funny. He had taken my hand and kept looking up at me as if I were a long lost relative. I thought he might be Hispanic so I tried the very few Spanish words I knew.

"*Donde esta Mama?*" Nothing but another giggle.

"Okay little fellow," I told him. "Let's look around. *Someone* must be missing you." How could anyone *not* be looking for this delightful and happy child.

Our first stop was the liquor store, where the few customers were stocking up on beer for the day's sporting events. They looked at us curiously when I asked if anyone had lost a child, but no one made any comments. The shopkeeper gave me some tissues for the child's runny nose, but other than that, no one had much interest in solving my problem. I decided to take one last look in a nearby fast-food restaurant before calling the police. But no one was looking for a lost boy there either. By now, about 45 minutes had passed and the little fellow was still laughing and making happy unintelligible sounds. He never let go of my hand throughout all this time.

"Okay, little guy," I informed him. "Time I called the police, unless of course you'd rather come to my house. What do you think? You could have a lot of fun with the crew who live in my place." I could just hear them now as I walked in the door.

"Hi Mom, did you get the milk? You go to the store and come home with a *kid!!"*

The kid, as if reading my mind, giggled again as he did over everything I said, though he obviously had no understanding of a word of it. So I went ahead and called the police thinking kidnapping was probably not a wise move to make. Within five minutes a police officer arrived. He was a big man with a handlebar mustache and many shiny keys, buttons and badges all over his uniform. It took my little friend all of three seconds to completely change his allegiance to this much more interesting person. The cop knew some Spanish, so he started asking the child where he lived and what his name was. Each question was greeted with a giggle but not a word in response.

"Officer, if no one claims him, could he come home with me? Just for a little while until you figure things out?" I asked sheepishly.

"Sorry Ma'am," was the quick reply. "He'll go into protective custody until we find the parents." I had a fleeting image of the little boy thrown into a holding cell with teenagers sporting nose rings, chains and purple hair.

"Before I take him to Children's Services though, I'll just take one last look for a relative." The little boy, without a backwards glance in my direction,

7

put his hand into the police officer's and gladly went off with his new friend.

As they were walking towards the fast food restaurant, I suddenly saw a slight young man coming down a flight of wooden steps from an apartment behind the liquor store. He was intently watching the policeman's back, but stopped several times on the steps as if unsure of what to do.
"Officer," I yelled out, "this might be the father."
The cop turned around, still holding the boy's hand.
"*Papa?*" he asked.
"*Si*," the man answered, though somewhat reluctantly.
"And *Mama?*" asked the police officer. The man pointed back up the stairs.
"OK. Let's go," said the cop, and all three started climbing the stairs. Not a word was said to me as they disappeared from view and headed into the apartment.

By now I was feeling pretty let down. I probably would never know what happened, why the parents hadn't missed this child for more than an hour, whether he would be taken from them as a case of child neglect, or if they would be deported if they proved to be undocumented. I was also pretty sure no one in the local police department would answer any of my questions. I didn't even know that lovely child's name and probably would never see him again. On top of that, by now my challah had more than likely risen completely over the bowl and was working its way along the counter toward the floor. I didn't even have the energy to go back to the store and buy the milk.

So, I headed to my car. It was a very warm day, and when I got in I could not touch the burning steering wheel. I rolled down the window and sat

8

there mulling over the events of the morning. Just then, there was a loud thump on the roof of the car. A disheveled looking man poked his head in my window and peered intently at me. I had not seen him approach and could not imagine where he had come from. I found myself gravitating to the passenger side of the car, so frightening did he appear. He had piercing black eyes, long dirty gray hair and two large gaps where top and bottom teeth should have been. He wore a dark coat-like garment with fraying cuffs, despite the day's heat. His hands, resting on the door of the car, were gnarled and the nails filthy. For a moment there was complete silence. Then his face softened and he said in a clear voice I remember to this day: "My faith in humanity has been restored today." Then he shuffled off without another word.

I sat there stunned. Who was this strange man and how did he know what had just transpired? In all the time I had been with the child I had never seen this frightening creature anywhere. And then I began to wonder if I had just come face to face with Eliahu HaNavi, Elijah the prophet. In one legend Elijah dresses as a beggar and wanders the earth looking for people in need of help. Maybe, I thought, that really was Elijah watching over the little boy. That thought never seemed more vivid to me than when sitting in the car considering the morning's extraordinary events.

I smiled to myself, and then I started the car to go home to my family, and to begin to get ready for Rosh Hashanah, the Jewish New Year.

*A version of "Eliahu HaNavi" appeared in the magazine Women's League Outlook, Vol. 69, No 1. Fall 1998.*

# Kol Nidrei

In the early morning light, Leah gingerly held on to the still flapping trout, careful to keep her thumb away from the hook's sharp point. She looked behind her and smiled tenderly at the sleeping forms of her brother and sister in the small copse of trees they had found last night. It was her nine year old brother Jacob's job to catch the fish, but she just couldn't get him motivated, as hungry as they were on this unending journey. The gentle rise and fall of six year old Rachel's tiny body belied the uneasy peacefulness around them.

Everything had gone wrong when their father, Yosef, had tripped over a loose axe in the shed and badly gashed his foot. Before that unfortunate event he had spent countless hours planning their escape into the forest. It was Yosef's hope that they find a partisan group there that would willingly take in all four of them. Their situation had become more urgent with each passing day, as dire reports were filtering into their village. The Nazis were rounding up and murdering Jews all around them. He knew it was just a matter of days now before their town would be overrun. Leah's desperate cajoling and pleading for the children to stay with their father fell on deaf ears.

"You must leave with your brother and sister, Leah. And now. There's *no* other choice."

He didn't tell Leah that a lack of any proper medical attention had caused a serious infection in his foot, making travel for him now virtually impossible. His instructions for living in the forest took on far more urgency, now that the children would be without him on their journey.

"Always stay close to the river. Be on alert at all times and plan to quickly get to a hiding place if you hear voices. Try to watch from a safe distance before making yourselves known. Leah, you'll need to be far smarter and wiser than you've ever been before." He turned away, but not before she saw tears on his cheek at the unbearable choice he was being forced to make.

Prior to his accident, Yosef had quite enjoyed teaching the children about the food they could gather and the mostly harmless forest animals they might encounter. Luckily sightings of wolves in their region of this vast forest were not that common. During their many hikes, he had pointed out safe plants to eat, and showed them how to catch fish with only a small hook. Now, alone in this vast frightening expanse of trees, the children survived on fish, and on roots and berries that Leah prayed would do them no harm. At least the fish were safe to eat, she thought, though a devil to catch.

It was now mid September, according to the crude calendar Leah's father had drawn for her. They had been on their journey for three weeks and four days. Yosef had instructed her to cross off each day so she would always know the date. Leah wasn't sure why it mattered, but as an obedient daughter she tried to do all her father asked of her. This was especially true after the death of their mother two years before, when he naturally began to rely on her help to a much greater degree. A bad case of influenza had rapidly spread throughout their village taking their mother and Leah's newborn baby brother in its cruel grip. As time went on, it made her sad that she was finding it harder to remember the things she had so loved about her mother. Now in this unnerving forest, she had to somehow muster up enough strength of will to take on the role of both parents for her young siblings.

The trout was no longer flopping around, allowing her to extricate it from the hook without snagging her fingers. This one was a little larger than usual, cheering her up at the prospect that there might just be enough to share today. Perhaps she'd even have a small fire going and the fish cooking before the children woke up, she thought. After wrapping up the hook and carefully putting it back in Jacob's satchel, Leah next pulled out the matchbox from a deep pocket in her own knapsack. But alarmingly there were only six matches left. Her father had given her very detailed instructions about when and where she could safely light a fire, and she had carefully followed his directions. But now she reluctantly faced the fact that she hadn't been so careful with the matches he provided. That thought of their life without matches was far too troubling for Leah's young mind to begin to contemplate.

Now she began gathering sticks and pine cones for the fire. They had been lucky in that the usual fall rains had held off since they left the village, keeping the plentiful fuel dry and easy to burn. Her father had made her practice many times over, building fires as small as possible so that the smoke would be minimal and wouldn't give away their hiding place. Papa, she thought, I know you want us to stay hidden. But also to find people to take us in. How can I do that myself, Papa? Can't you help us? Where *are* you?

While the fish was sizzling in the pan, she cheered herself up a bit by pulling out her father's primitive calendar from a section of her bag where she kept her prized possessions. There was her mother's ornate silver

12

brooch her father had given her on the day they left, a faded photo from her parents' wedding day, and one of her best friend Mimi who disappeared one night several months ago with her parents and older brothers. Wherever they were going, thought Leah bitterly, there wasn't even enough time to say goodbye.

Leah picked up the calendar and searched next to the day's date to see if her father had written her an encouraging note. She loved getting his messages and, in fact, never looked ahead so that each new day she felt he was right there speaking to her in person. Today, though, she saw something that puzzled her, as she couldn't immediately understand what her father meant. Next to the date he had written two Hebrew letters: Koof and Nun. But in the next moment it dawned on Leah that he wanted her to know tonight was Kol Nidrei, one of the holiest nights of the year when Jews all over the world gathered to collectively atone for their sins.

Yosef had never been particularly religious, but there were some things that were very important to him, and one of those was observing Kol Nidrei, the start of the twenty-four hour fasting period when Yom Kippur, the Day of Atonement, officially began. In fact, early every summer, in his booming baritone voice and to the eternal mortification of his wife and children, the entire village could hear him singing the ancient haunting melody. That particular tune, known simply as Kol Nidrei, was familiar to most Jews no matter what their personal observance. It became a standard joke in the village that Yosef had so many sins to atone for, he had to start preparing months in advance of everyone else! His children would roll their eyes, but often they found themselves smiling and singing along with him. This past summer, when Leah had turned twelve, her father told her she could try fasting for the very first time in observance of the holiday.

13

"Now every day seems to be a fast day, Papa," she whispered bitterly to herself, as she watched the sizzling fish shrink a little from its original size.

After they had finished eating their breakfast, wrapping the remains for later and carefully dousing the fire, the children gathered their few belongings and started walking again on the crude path next to the river. Jacob was grumbling even more than usual about another long day of "useless" walking. Leah was desperately hoping that they might meet some partisans, and soon. But in the more than three weeks since they left the village they hadn't heard even one other human voice.

This particular day was bright and crisp, but Leah knew they didn't have a lot of time before cold nights hit them hard. Adding to their long list of difficulties, the sole of Rachel's left shoe was coming apart, and though her father had given them string for such emergencies, the last of it was badly fraying and probably wouldn't last another day.

Towards mid afternoon, as they continued to walk along the bank of the meandering river, they came upon a small clearing. Leah had been carrying Rachel on her back for the last hour and knew she couldn't go any further without a rest.
"Let's take a short nap before we find a place to settle for the night," she suggested as she gently put Rachel down.

When Leah awoke several hours later, she realized the evening had started to creep up on them and they would now have to stay where they were for the night. They would need to look for berries soon, she thought, with a resigned sigh at the monotony their daily life had become. The children were still asleep curled up next to each other. She got up and began to walk towards the river, hoping a long drink would stave off this unrelenting hunger for a few more hours.

Suddenly from a grove of trees on the other side of the clearing, she heard the sound of sticks cracking. So far they had escaped the rare but always dreaded wolves. She wondered, though, if their luck might have run out tonight. Very quietly she walked closer to where she heard the noise and crouched down so as not to be seen. There through the trees she could just make out the outline of a man and woman who were now talking quietly in Yiddish, but loud enough for her to hear.

"Isaac," asked the young woman, "when does Mika relieve you? You've been out here for hours."

"Soon, Sarah," he replied. "Ssh, what's that sound? Stay here while I go take a look."

Leah's entire body started shaking with fear. She didn't believe her father's unconditional assurances that a group of Jewish partisans would welcome children without an accompanying adult. Deep down Leah knew they might still be on their own no matter how much she pleaded. Her choice was to take her chances with this group, or somehow try to find their way back to the village. And what if we do get back there and Papa is nowhere to be found, she argued with herself. Maybe there's no one left. Then what. That was an eventuality she couldn't bear to think about. Leah also knew that staying in the forest by themselves was no longer a viable option.

But then, just as suddenly, a peacefulness settled over her entire being, as she remembered this was a very special evening. She thought about the Kol Nidrei service in happier times when her family and all the members of their village gathered together in a small wooden synagogue at the center of the town square. With that memory giving her sustenance, she stood up straight and began to walk towards the grove of trees from where the young man and woman had just emerged. As she walked towards the couple, in her clear and beautiful voice she sang the words of the ancient haunting melody,

"Kol Nidrei, v'esarei, vaharamei......"

She heard people behind the trees calling to each other, "Do you hear that? Is that a child singing Kol Nidrei? Is tonight the start of Yom Kippur?"

And one by one the band of tired and hungry resisters emerged from their hiding places. Soon someone joined Leah's singing, and then another holding a child's hand began humming the melody. Jacob and Rachel, awakened by the sounds around them, had come to stand on either side of Leah and each had taken one of her hands. They too joined the chorus of whispering voices. For a moment Leah stopped and looked up to glimpse the moon shining brightly above her through the canopy of trees. Suddenly an incredible lightness of spirit entered her heart, giving her the strength to carry on. And then with a spontaneous cry of joy, the three children began running towards the group that was coming towards them.

# A Chance Encounter

"This heat is unbearable," Rena thought as she sat on a wall outside the large plantation house, now a museum in South Carolina. Her husband, Jack, was at that moment part of a tour walking around the former slave quarters. "You go ahead," she told him. "I'll wander around the museum shop for a while." In truth, she couldn't bring herself to go into this section of the plantation but she wasn't sure Jack would understand.

Rena had retired from her thirty-year job as a Social Worker for Jewish Family Services in San Francisco. She and Jack decided to take their first tour of the deep South to see for themselves where battles had been fought, slaves held and sold, and civil rights marchers arrested. "Why don't you pick somewhere cooler?" their concerned daughter, Melanie, had asked. Now, Rena was beginning to think maybe Melanie had been right all along.

Rena pulled herself up slowly, wiped her brow with a tissue, and headed over to the museum shop to kill some time while waiting for Jack. It proved to be a good decision as this, at least, was an air conditioned space providing some relief from the oppressive humidity. The shop had only a few browsers walking around as she headed in. It was full of large posters of fairly well known artists Rena recalled seeing on the main house tour. It was also replete with curios that one might have found in the best of houses during the early to mid-nineteenth century, all now made in China but, nevertheless, meant to conjure up a whole different world. Sewing kits, strange kinds of kitchen utensils, fans and hats from that era were artfully spread around the shop, enticing tourists to part with their cash. She examined one piece after another and then stopped suddenly, a little surprised by what she *wasn't* seeing.

Sitting near a cash register up front was a very blond and tightly coiffed middle aged woman pouring over some wares and putting little price tags on them. Rena walked over to the woman and looked at her name tag which announced Barbara Volunteer. Rena waited for Barbara Volunteer to notice she was standing at the counter. After a few moments she cleared her throat loudly and the woman looked up and flushed a little.

"Oh, I'm so sorry," she drawled. "I didn't notice you there. How can I help you?" and then she flashed her most gracious smile of encouragement as if to say: "Isn't there something here you want to buy? It hasn't been a great day in the sales department."

"I was wondering," Rena began, a little tentative at first that she was even asking the question. "I notice your shop is full of lovely art and knickknacks but not a thing that tells us this was once a *slave* plantation. Weren't there any pieces of pottery or ceramics, maybe created by those residents showing that hundreds of African men, women and children were held here as chattel?" She felt her own face redden and her voice rise as the indignity of the situation hit her.

Barbara flushed easily, only this time it was obvious she was not embarrassed - she was angry.

"Well, I'm just a volunteer here and don't select the inventory."

Now it was Rena's turn to be angry. "You mean *inventory* like the slaves were when, no doubt, people just like you were running places like this one!"

Rena realized she was unfairly attacking this woman, who after all, was just doing her civic duty, but she couldn't stop her rage. The heat, the injustice and cruelty of the period, and even a little anger directed at Jack that

18

apparently he didn't feel the same sense of outrage as she as he had chosen to go on the tour. She felt it all conspiring against her at that moment.

"I'll have to ask you to leave if you can't lower your voice," Barbara admonished Rena.

"Why? Are you afraid someone might hear my question?" asked Rena as she stalked away in disgust. She was a short stocky woman but her booming voice when she was angry somehow made her sound like a much larger person. Years of listening to angry parents and their children, bureaucrats, and others had taken their toll on her and often caused her to lash out when she shouldn't have. She didn't like this side of herself but couldn't seem to make it go away either.


Now as she headed towards the back of the shop to give it one last look, a young woman of perhaps thirty years of age approached her.

"I heard what you said and I was thinking the same thing. If you hadn't asked the question I was going to, although maybe a little gentler!" The woman was tall and very slim with long strands of cornrows that clicked together as she moved her head.

"Do you mind if I ask you," asked Rena "how long that process takes?"

"What?" asked the young woman.

"Oh, getting your hair to look like that?"

"About eight hours!" laughed the young woman, at this obvious non sequitur having nothing to do with the apparent outrage they both were feeling.

"Wow, it's beautiful but looks painful! I hope you didn't mind my asking you that question."

"Not at all. It's very common for white women to be fascinated by our cornrows!"

"Are you from around here?" Rena asked, not wishing to end the conversation right away.

"No I'm living in Cleveland now but I had a week off and thought I'd take a look at some history. I went on the plantation tour earlier but couldn't bring myself to see the slave quarters."

"Me neither," admitted Rena, already feeling a camaraderie with this young woman and liking it. "I shouldn't have yelled at that woman though. I do that too much. I'm actually waiting for my husband who *is* on the tour. This is our first trip outside of San Francisco in a very long time since I just retired."

"Oh, well congratulations on your retirement. I lived in San Francisco myself for a few years and just loved the city!" replied the young woman.

"Were you working there too?" asked Rena.

"No. Actually I was a medical student at UCSF and was extremely lucky to get a cardiology residency at Case Western. Once I start that in a few weeks, I can forget about any kind of life for three years," she laughed. She had a pleasant and warm laugh that lit up her beautiful face.

Rena felt herself becoming uncomfortable, afraid she might say the wrong thing and embarrass herself and this young woman. How hard, she wondered, was it for an African American woman to get into such a prestigious medical school? And then she silently berated herself for having the thought at all. If this had been a young white man that question would never have even popped into my head, now would it, she wondered? Deep down, am I as bigoted as Barbara's ancestors, and am I really just an armchair liberal? How many African Americans can I count among my friends? None, if truth be told. I was never really friends with any of my black work colleagues, although I liked them well enough. Our lives just traveled different paths. In fact, she thought, living in this area it's not unlikely that Barbara may have some African American acquaintances, perhaps even friends. These fleeting thoughts troubled Rena greatly.

Giving her head a quick shake as if to clear it, Rena started to walk over to where the young woman was now looking at a large art book. She had moved over to the book section, apparently when she figured their brief conversation was over.

"Do you mind if I ask you something? I'm Rena, by the way."

"And I'm Michelle."

"If it's not too rude of me, Michelle, can you tell me how you really feel today? It's one thing for me to understand how I feel, but how can you bear to come here?"

"Well, let me explain something, Rena. My father was in the army and when I was a teenager he was posted to an army base in Germany. During that year we traveled quite extensively in Europe and, on one trip to Poland, we actually went to Auschwitz, the Nazi concentration camp. Do you know about it?"

"Yes, unfortunately, I know all about it. I'm Jewish," answered Rena.

"Oh," Michelle said, "then of course it's an unbearable part of your history. There was a group of Jewish American teenagers, about my age at the time, on the same tour. I wondered how they could step foot inside the camp. So I asked one young girl that same question you just asked me, and she said simply: 'If we don't remember then we're doomed to forget'. This of course is not an original idea, but seemed to be her own adopted mantra though. That's how I feel being here today. Funny, though, my father insisted we walk through the crematorium at Auschwitz but I couldn't bring myself to go to the slave quarters here.

"Have you ever wondered what is worse - an entire life condemned to slavery or a quick death in the gas chambers? One could argue that at least the slaves had some kind of a life, however harsh it was. And they always had the hope of freedom one day. These are such difficult questions, aren't they?" she asked Rena.

"Do you think," Rena asked, "if we were all required to visit a slave plantation, a crematorium, the Holocaust museum, or something showing man's incredible inhumanity to man, we'd all be more compassionate?"

"I don't really know. Maybe if women - mothers - ran the world it would be less cruel. But there were lots of women guards in the camps and lots of women slave owners were as cruel to 'their property' as their husbands. It's so hard to remain hopeful in the face of such absolute brutality we see even today, isn't it?" asked Michelle. "But, by nature, I'm an optimist and what keeps me going is that there are so many more really good people than bad ones. Unfortunately, they don't make the news headlines nearly enough though."

"You are wise beyond your years, Michelle. I must admit when I was your age I wasn't thinking thoughts like these!"

"Comes with having a father who made us think about the big picture and outside the box. It wasn't always easy being his daughter but I'm glad he made us look at how others lived, and sometimes even at how they died too. I'd like to think it made my brother and me better people, somehow having the luck of the draw with the parents we got. In a way this trip for me is a tribute to my dad. He died just six months ago - of a heart attack."

Rena wondered if their own daughter, Melanie, ever thought about Jack and her with any kind of obvious veneration. Probably not, was her sad conclusion.

At that moment Rena saw Jack come into the shop and wave. She held up her hand, giving him a sign to wait a moment for her. She saw him nod his head in assent, and then move over to a sale table near the front of the store.

"Michelle," said Rena, "I'm going to have to go. Would it be okay if I gave you my contact information? I know you're going to be incredibly busy, but maybe we could keep in touch now and then?" she asked hopefully.

"Yes, I'd like that very much, Rena. There's a conference coming up in San Francisco I'm hoping to attend next spring, so maybe we can get together for lunch one day if I make it out West." They pulled out their phones so that they could exchange each other's contact information.

On impulse Rena put her arms around the much taller woman and gave her a tight hug before going to join her husband. As she walked away she felt a tear trickle down her face. Why, she couldn't exactly say, but at that very moment she knew her heart was full.

# The Highwayman

Cigar ash dropped to the shelf created by Harry's protruding belly, but he didn't seem to notice. Sitting on his porch late that Sunday afternoon, he was too busy deciding which of his three Caddies, parked with their smiling grills facing him, he would drive tomorrow. To the side of where the cars were located, and stretching for about a quarter of a mile, was a long and straight dirt road leading from the front of his house to Rural Route 3 up ahead.

Harry owned the only car repair business for miles, located in Mayfield about 20 minutes from his home. He liked to tell anyone who would listen about how his grandfather had built that garage, almost as soon as Mr. Ford's first cars came down the assembly line. Now approaching his 60th year, Harry regularly wondered what would happen to the business when he finally decided to retire. He had never married and had few relatives he wanted to see, let alone leave a thriving business to one of them.

Lost in thought as he was, it was not surprising that Harry didn't immediately notice a plume of dust rising from the access road, gradually moving nearer to his house. He waited in the old lounge chair, puffing on his cigar and wondered if it was that useless mechanic, Joe, coming to ask for tomorrow off. But as the car approached, Harry could tell it was long and sleek and definitely not Joe's ancient Chevy truck.

The driver slowed and then stopped next to Flo, Harry's cherished '56 sky blue Caddie. He had bought Flo brand new almost 10 years ago now, but she still retained that new car look and smell. The door of the strange car

24

(to his annoyance, Harry couldn't identify the make) slowly opened and a tall, slim and dark skinned man stepped out.

Now one thing we need to clarify about Harry right at the outset is that he was not in favor, no Siree, of any of President Johnson's lame-brained ideas, one of which was to allow black people to sit in restaurants next to him, or to mess up the schools that were working just fine, thank you very much, *without* Lyndon's meddling. As far as Harry was concerned, black people should know their place, and that did not include coming nonchalantly towards his front porch. However due to Harry's excessive weight, at this particular moment he was prevented from getting out of his chair and confronting this unwelcome visitor from an upright position.

"Just a moment, Mr. Sherman," the visitor held his hand up as if to stop Harry from even trying to get up. The man looked to be in his mid forties, had a full head of curly white hair and carried himself with a self-assurance Harry was not used to seeing in others, especially not in black people. He wore a smart white three piece suit, white shirt and silk tie, and white buckskin shoes. The only noticeable color on him was a ruby-studded tie pin.

"Please let me explain why I'm here. I just need a few moments of your time, if you'll allow me." He had a funny way of enunciating every word, as if he were teaching a class in Shakespearean drama.
"I have a lot to do and don't have time to be talkin' with someone I ain't never met before. And how do you know my name, anyway?" Harry asked impatiently, while simultaneously trying unsuccessfully to block the stranger from advancing any further on his porch.

"My name is Angel," said the man with an outstretched hand, "and I've been sent on a mission by Him to talk to you."

"Who's Him?" asked Harry, rudely ignoring Angel's hand.

"You know. *The* Him." Mr. Angel pointed upwards and smiled showing beautiful even white teeth.

"You just wait a minute! I ain't got time for no Bible thumpers. I'll thank you to move along and get that there car off of my property."

By this time Mr. Angel was on the porch, and in fact was pulling another old chair right next to Harry's as if the two of them were lifelong buddies.

"Now Mr. Sherman, you and I need to have a nice chat."

"I'm calling the Sheriff if you're not off of my porch in 10 seconds or less. Got that?"

"Remember that '57 Dodge belonging to poor widow Riley?" continued Mr. Angel, completely unfazed by the interruptions. "And the '62 Corvair Mary Sue's son Jack brought in? And what about that VW bus those hippie girls, Daisy and Rose, brought by just last week?"

Harry's eyes grew wide as he held up a hand to stop Mr. Angel. "You from the State or somethin'? I pay my taxes on time every year."

"Well, yes. I'm from *His* State. Now pay attention to what He's proposing and why I was sent to talk to you. We are very much aware, Mr. Sherman, that the transmission on Widow Riley's Dodge just needed a servicing, but you managed to charge her for an entirely *new* transmission. And those hippie girls only needed their tires rotated, not to be sold four brand new ones, isn't that right, Mr. Sherman? It took every last bit of cash they had to pay you for those wheels. Are you getting my drift, Mr. Sherman? We have been keeping tabs on you for the last five years, and frankly, as your Account Manager, I've been getting mighty troubled by these observations. In fact when He and I" -once again the upward pointing of the finger- "heard Jennie Mae and her elderly mother talking about that Ford

Edsel...now of course we are aware of other problems with the Edsel, but that's neither here nor there. What I'm talking about is *you* telling Jennie Mae that the steering column was off-kilter and could cause a problem if it wasn't replaced, when it wasn't a problem at all. Over five years, Mr. Sherman, we have been keeping a close record, all written down for Posterity" - here Mr. Angel chuckled at his own joke though Harry was not amused- "and know about each and every one of your egregious transgressions."

"Who the hell are you?" Harry's eyes were fairly popping out of his now ashen face during Mr. Angel's monologue.
"That's an unfortunate choice of words, Harry. May I call you Harry? I feel like we're going to become very good friends soon, don't you?"
"What do you want? Money? I'll give you ... um..... $100 right now and we need never talk about this again."
"No, no Harry. You're missing the point. Harry, Harry, twenty years of ripping off poor uneducated folks... about cars that is. That has got to be addressed. You see this all came to a head last week when .... Let's see.."
Mr. Angel pulled a tiny notebook and pair of half glasses out of his pocket. Turning some pages in the notebook he found what he was looking for.

"Yes, here it is. It was Mary Beth Todd. One night she was having a conversation with Him. She told Him she didn't like to ask for much but she really needed a car so she could get to her classes at the College. And be able to get home every night to stay with her ailing mother. He granted her wish, but then do you remember what happened next? You, Harry, knowingly sold her a lemon you had on your lot. That's the car that you took, illegally I might add, from Mike Watson, when he couldn't pay for the first round of repairs. This car was in desperate need of major work,

27

remember that? We saw you rubbing your hands together with glee when you sold her that worthless heap of junk and then" - Mr. Angel stopped for effect for a moment and then leaned in for the kill - "we saw you change the odometer from 150,000 to 20,000 miles just before Mary Beth picked it up. Needless to say, we were extremely sad when Mary Beth had to spend a week in the hospital after her accident. I hesitate to think what might have been the end for that poor unfortunate girl, on that slick road when the brakes failed, if He hadn't stepped in."

"Oh my God," cried Harry, though in truth *He* wasn't particularly sympathetic to the call at that moment. This time Harry successfully pushed himself out of the chair, but he lost his balance due to the momentum, and landed heavily on the porch.

"Please Mr. Angel, don't send me to burn in Hell for eternity. I'll do anything. Please, please I'll be good from now on. I promise." Harry was clutching at Mr. Angel's leg and sobbing uncontrollably.

"OK, Harry. You can get up now. It's time to talk business."

With much effort Harry raised himself up, took a kerchief from his pocket and began mopping his brow with a shaky hand. He got back in the chair and turned his full attention to Mr. Angel.

"OK, I'm listening," he sighed.

"Good, Harry, because here's the plan we've come up with. You will have to carry out every part of it, no cutting corners. Do you understand?"

At this point Harry felt he would agree to anything. That is, until he heard the first demand.

"Number one, Harry, you will turn your entire business over to Joe..."

"No! You mean *give* it to that nincompoop?"

"That is correct. And by the way he's a very intelligent and kind man, Harry, with something you have no idea about - it's called morals. Next you will give Miss Jennie Mae and her mother your house and everything in it."

"No way am I going to let them live in my house! They're bla….." Harry stopped himself in time and thought better of what he was about to say.

Mr. Angel continued ignoring each and every one of Harry's interruptions. "The family of the Widow Riley will get your three Cadillacs. Mrs. Riley has three wonderful grandsons, all upstanding young men we've been watching. We know they will make amazing contributions to this Great Society President Johnson has been talking to Him about for the last few years. And we have complete confidence they will take care of the cars just as you do now."

"Oh no, please not my Caddies, they're my very special ladies. Could I at least keep Flo?" Harry was blubbering and whining like a baby now.

"No, all three have to go. Alright Harry, the decision is in your hands now," said Mr. Angel preparing to get up.

"Ok, Ok. Please don't tell me there's more."

"You will buy a small van with room inside for a bed, a stove and all the tools you will need," continued Mr. Angel, though he was beginning to tire of this exceedingly troublesome mortal.

"Tools for what?" asked Harry incredulously.

"To fix cars of course," answered Mr. Angel. "You will paint 'The Highwayman' on the side of your van and for the next 10 years you will drive the highways and byways of America. Whenever you see anyone in trouble, you will stop and fix their car, at no charge of course. You will never ever pass a driver in need of help. I will check in every now and then but you should know we will always be watching you day and night."

"You're kidding! Ten years. And look at me! Tell me do I look like anyone who can bend down to change tires? Joe does most all the repairs - well not the stuff I take care of. Couldn't trust him not to quit or call in the law if I asked him to take on some of my special projects." Harry's voice trailed off with the realization of what he had just owned up to.

"Well glad to hear you recognize Joe's contribution to the success of your business! And yes, I do notice your ...ahem.... physical condition," commented Mr. Angel, looking down once again at Harry's enormous girth. "You'll just have to figure out how to lose that weight so you can do your job. We can't give you every answer, Harry. You do still have that thing called 'Free Will'. But here's an idea that is bound to help. Every day right before breakfast, you should do a calisthenics program designed by Yours Truly. I do it religiously myself, and look what good shape I'm in for someone who is 783 years old?"

Harry didn't like any part of this plan and was still looking for an out.

"And how do I pay for this plan of yours, O master of all the answers?" he asked a bit sharply he realized, though he'd had enough of Mr. Angel by this point.

"Oh we both know you have bags of money stashed away. And as your Account Manager I'll be watching the balance sheet very closely."

"When do I start - if I decide to go ahead?" asked Harry.

"Well, let's see." Once again Mr. Angel pulled out his little notebook. "Today is Sunday. How about two weeks from today? That should be plenty of time to put your affairs in order."

"And if I refuse....?"

"I don't think so Harry. The alternative is not a pretty picture. Nope, not a pretty picture at all." He sighed and shook his shock of curls for emphasis. But then he smiled, knowing that he was about to be free of this tiresome human, for a few weeks anyway.

"And now Harry, I'm off to Liverpool to get autographs from those Four lads -- once I figure out how to get around all those screaming girls. Bye now."

Mr. Angel rose gracefully from the chair, walked to his car and with a wave of his hand took off down the road.

Harry watched for a moment as the dust rose once again in the car's wake. "Nah," he said, shaking his head. "Couldn't be true. Just one of them optical illusions. I won't remember none of this nightmare tomorrow. Now let's just see, where should I go for dinner tonight? Think I fancy myself a steak at Ma Kelly's."

Suddenly Harry's eye caught something glinting on the porch, shining brightly in the light of the fading sun. With grunts and heaves he bent down to see what it was. Caught in the grooves of the wood was a small ruby-studded tie pin. Harry picked it up, and with a resigned sigh slipped it in his pocket, to be returned to Mr. Angel when next they met.

# Marcos

The clock on the wall glowed 4:12 in my darkened room. A slightly ajar door showed some light, but there was a curtain at the end of my bed obstructing the view into the hallway. I could see rubber-soled shoes going back and forth, and snippets of conversations drifted back to me.

"I don't think Mr. Sandoval in 152 is going to make it, do you?"
"Do you think I should break up with Mike?"
"I can't believe Joanne gave me this lousy shift again…"

This was my first overnight stay in a hospital and I was finding sleeping in this environment to be an oxymoron. Each medical resident who awakened me during the night asked basically the same questions. I wondered why such brilliant people couldn't just read a person's medical chart and leave him alone, especially in the middle of the night. You're being unfair, I argued with myself. How else can they learn? But couldn't they do their studying during daylight hours, I argued back again?

Was it just yesterday afternoon when I had had that horrible sensation in my chest? I remember Miles, Yuki and I were in the conference room arguing vociferously about the Tyson wrongful termination case. Yuki and I wanted to recommend a settlement but Miles, the senior partner, thought we should let it go to trial. Suddenly I found I couldn't catch my breath and the pain in my left arm and shoulder was unbearable as I slid off my chair to the floor. I heard someone yell "I think Benjamin's having a heart attack. Quick, call 911!"

I must have passed out, because the next thing I remember was waking up in a moving ambulance with wires attached and an oxygen mask over my face. Several paramedics peered at me closely and rattled off numbers to each other. It all felt very ethereal, like I was watching myself on an old episode of *ER*. At one point, one of the paramedics asked me if there was anyone who should be notified, so they could meet me at the hospital.

To my horror I felt a tear slide down my face.

My ex-wife, Shira, lived in Seattle. And our only child, Daniel, had just graduated from Duke and was traveling with a school buddy through Nepal. For as long as I could remember Daniel had had a fascination with the Himalayas and at this moment was probably at some base camp or another. Newsy bits appeared with regularity on Facebook, but writing those special emails to his dad were few and far between.

As to friends and relatives? We didn't have any local relatives and it had been complicated with friends. Most of our friends were married couples who weren't really sure how to relate to each of us separately. Even with Shira living elsewhere, they certainly hadn't made much effort to keep in touch with me. I sensed their discomfort when I called, so after a while I stopped and put all my energy into work.

"No," I whispered to the paramedic behind my mask. "No one to contact right now. Maybe later."

They put me in a private corner room in the CICU, which I later discovered stood for Cardiac Intensive Care Unit. It was a pleasant room as hospital rooms go, overlooking a patio full of lush green plants brushing up against the window. Shortly after I arrived, the attending physician gave me a thorough exam, ordered some tests, pronounced my color good, but said little else. He seemed unusually rushed as his attention kept going to the door. He did say I would probably be out in a few days as it didn't look like any major damage had been done, but we obviously needed to wait for the cardiologist's report. Encouraging news which helped cheer me up a bit.

The nursing staff was efficient but very busy with more serious cases, so I was left in the hands of the medical interns for the most part. Later in the day I received some concerned calls from work, but politely declined their offer to visit or bring me anything. And when a kindly volunteer came by pushing a book cart, I chose a John Grisham novel I had somehow missed when it first made its appearance a few years earlier.

At 5:30 that morning I picked up the book again, knowing the night was done for me, and became engrossed until breakfast arrived. The rest of the morning was spent on tests with respiratory and EKG technicians who efficiently did their work. I felt encouraged by their smiles and almost jovial enthusiasm about how well I was doing. The morning, however, was punctuated by intermittent crying from a nearby room, and I would momentarily wonder about the patient, but then just as quickly forgot as I got deeper into Mr. Grisham's thriller.

After lunch, Cindy, one of the more friendly members of the team, told me I had to get up and walk around. I was delighted as I am a very active person and lying in bed for hours is not my idea of fun. Cindy made sure the IV's were properly hooked up for my stroll. I, on the other hand, was much more concerned about the opening in the back of my hospital gown! She handed me another to wear, and modesty was restored, at least for the moment. Cindy pointed me down the hall towards a visitor's room which she felt would provide a nice change of venue.

Shuffling down the hall in my hospital gown and slippers and dragging along the IV pole, I must say made me feel like an old sick man, though in reality I am barely forty-five. But it did feel good and a relief that my breathing felt regular and even.

The visitor's room served not only as a change of venue for patients, but a place where their family and friends could sit and talk in more comfortable surroundings. It was a bright room facing the patio with ivory walls, printed couches and chairs with colorful matching cushions. Magazines were spread out on low tables, and there were several vending machines along the walls, and a huge flat screen TV that dominated the room.

The only occupant was a teenage boy hunched up on one of the chairs, apparently engrossed in a baseball game on the TV. He had light brown skin, longish straight black hair and wore green shorts, beat up tennis shoes with only one lace between them, and a yellow tee shirt with a pronounced hole in the shoulder seam. He looked to be about fourteen or so, though I'm not very good at telling the age of children.

"Hi," I said as I came further into the room.

He didn't look up or answer for a beat and then said in a low voice:

"They said my dad might die today or tomorrow, I don't know." There was little inflection to his voice, but the TV remote control going nervously from one hand to the other told a different story.

I felt a shock wave go through me, more identifying with the patient than sympathizing with the boy at that moment. That must have been where the wailing was coming from, I realized.

"He got a heart attack on Monday - it was real bad." And again: "He ain't going to make it - they can't fix his heart." A hand came up to brush away a tear I wasn't meant to see. I approached and, after some negotiating with the IV pole, took a seat opposite within his line of vision. He looked up, as if really noticing me for the first time.

"What's wrong wid you?" he asked in that direct no-nonsense way kids have.

"They think I had a slight heart attack yesterday. But I'll be fine. Going home in a few days, I think." I meant it as kind of a reassurance to him that people do get better. But the kid wasn't having any of it.

"Not my dad. They can't get a new heart in time. We got insurance and everythin', but they still can't find a heart. Bet they could if he was a rich white guy," he added bitterly looking directly at me. I was about to tell him that didn't make any difference, but then I hesitated because frankly I wasn't really sure.

"Do you mind if we turn down the TV, sorry what's your name….?"

"Marcos," he muttered reluctantly as if I had no right to this information.

"I'm Benjamin," I added, as he acquiesced and turned the volume down slightly.

After a few minutes with both of us quietly watching the half time antics of jumping girls and silly mascots, he asked "Do you got any money?" eyeing the vending machines.

I had had the presence of mind to slip my wallet into a pocket I found in the gown. No point in tempting fate by leaving it in an empty room.

"Sure, here," I offered, taking out a ten dollar bill. "Sorry I don't have anything smaller."

"You want somethin'?" he asked as he pulled out a soda from one machine and two candy bars from another.

36

"Thanks but I better not," I said as I made hand motions in the neighborhood of my heart. A slight smile washed over his face before he caught it and went all serious again. I thought he might pocket the change but he brought it over to me and I took it so as not to embarrass him.

"We've been here a lot with my dad.... You know." His voice trailed off. Then he added by way of explanation, "My mom is pretty broken up and not thinking about food and stuff for us kids right now."

I said nothing. What could one say to a kid who was not only about to lose his father, but I suspected the family's main source of income too?

Despite the boy's fidgeting and tension, the room was so warm with the afternoon sun streaming in, that I felt my eyes drift closed. But not for long, apparently. I woke suddenly to a hand shaking my shoulder.

"Hey mister, you still alive?"

I opened my eyes to find Marcos peering at my face, obvious worry showing in his eyes. He smiled and said "Geez, I thought you was a goner!"

The first person to really care much in years, I thought ironically, is a skinny kid who doesn't know me from Adam.

After that we chatted more easily. He told me that his family of three kids and his parents lived with his aunt and uncle and their four children in a small rented house. Eleven people in one little house. Then I visualized a place bustling with laughter, loud meals, and occasional fights, and wondered what that would be like most of the time. The home we sold after the divorce had had five bedrooms for three people. There were days sometimes when we never really interacted much, each doing his own thing. Now I lived by myself in a comfortable and spacious condo. I was not so naive to believe I would ever want to live in a crowded and small home, but I did wonder what it would be like to live with a lot of people who cared for each other.

My thoughts drifted to Shira and what had gone wrong with our marriage. She had had a miserable pregnancy and difficult birth with Daniel. Afterwards it took her months to get over a bout of postpartum depression. She vowed that Daniel's would be the only birth she would endure. We talked about adoption when he was seven, but the truth is I wasn't really ready to take that plunge. Whenever Daniel asked why he couldn't have a brother or sister like all his friends did, Shira would pointedly look at me and tell him to ask his father.

And so we drifted apart trying to hide our growing apathy to each other from Daniel. Until one day Shira announced she was filing for divorce and was moving to Seattle where she could pursue her interest in art at a gallery there that had made her an offer of part time work. We saw each other at Daniel's graduations and she seemed happy with the choices she had made for herself.

"Hey Mister," Marcos broke into my reverie. "I better get back and see how my dad's doing."
"I'm ready to head back too. What room is your dad in?"
"152," he answered and then I remembered the nurse saying she didn't think Mr. Sandoval in 152 would make it. "What room you got?"
"147," I told him.
"You got anyone in there wid you?"
"No," I answered, wondering again how I had lucked out to get my own room.

"We got this old guy in there always making all kinds of noises, know what I mean?"

"Gees, that's got to be annoying," I sympathized, realizing I was falling naturally into his casual speech patterns and liking it. As we walked down the hall, Marcos slowed his pace so that I could keep abreast of him.

His father's room came before mine, and suddenly Marcos raced ahead. There was loud and piercing wailing filling the entire hallway. As I passed the open door, I glimpsed into a very crowded room with people alternatively hugging and crying. A nurse had her arm over the shoulder of a youngish woman near collapse. Marcos' mother I wondered. I was about to move on, feeling it rude to linger, when I saw Marcos sink to his knees with his head in his hands and body wracked with sobs. If I had died yesterday, I feel certain Daniel would have reacted the same way, but halfway around the world.

I went back to my room, deeply saddened by the scene I had just witnessed and pulled myself into bed. I must have fallen asleep because when I next awoke the clock on the wall registered 4:30 pm. I could hear much activity in the hallway, pointing to the fact that the staff was so busy they had left me alone for several hours. Then I noticed a piece of paper at the foot of my bed with some poorly scribbled writing on it. I reached down and picked it up. It said simply:

"Hey Mister hope you get better soon Marcos." On the back of the paper was the hospital menu for dinner that night, no longer needed by his dad.

I felt some tears well up thinking about this young boy who had just lost his father, but cared enough to write me a note. At that moment I resolved to find out where the family lived so I could pay them a call. And I would find out about those organizations that pair up kids like Marcos with guys

39

like me. Maybe I could even be a Big Brother to Marcos. I felt a smile envelope me as I looked ahead to a much brighter day!

# An Immigrant's Tale

I stumbled haltingly along an inner hallway of the violently rocking ship trying to keep my balance. It was dark and empty everywhere except for brown paper bags spaced at intervals along the floor. Although the worst of the storm had passed, many people were still experiencing recurring seasickness. Other than the constant creeping of the liner as it rolled back and forth, there was now just an eerie silence.

The perpetual droning of the engines had stopped sometime in the middle of the night as a tremendous Atlantic October storm hit suddenly with very little warning to the passengers, and now most of them were lying moaning or simply inert in their bunks. For some reason, my stomach had not lurched and heaved like that of my mother and little sister. Once awakened by the violence of the storm, I sat up most of that fateful night terrified that we would all drown at any moment. I could hear crew members through the wall of the cabin as they ran around the ship trying to deal with what we later heard was one emergency after another. For the most part, the passengers were forgotten and since movement was difficult and dangerous, most just stayed in their cabins. Unfortunately, since this was a Greek registered ship, I couldn't understand a word of what they were shouting at each other. It was only because of an incredible miracle, that that ship stayed upright throughout the night. And now in the morning, I managed to keep my balance by hanging onto the railing as I ascended to the next deck level hoping to find someone who could point the way to the kitchen.

Why the kitchen you might wonder? Well in her delirium from worry and seasickness, my mother wasn't thinking straight. She told me she had something very important for me to do for my little sister. In her terrified mind it seemed that if I didn't get oranges for my sister she would surely die of scurvy. Now of course everyone knows you can't get scurvy in a few days - sailors on ships for months were vulnerable but not after a few days at sea. But my otherwise competent and intelligent mother told me I had to find the kitchen and ask someone there to give me a bag of oranges. I remember looking over questionably at my 5 year old sister who at that very moment was going through some dry heaves again. How my mother imagined she could get oranges into her was a mystery, but I was an obedient child, so I put on my shoes and headed out the cabin door on a mission to save my sister's life.

We had left Cork, Ireland four days before, on what my mother thought was a luxury passenger liner to Canada. Oh how she and everyone else on that fateful ship had been duped. In my few short years I had traveled to Israel with my parents to live on a kibbutz, then back to Ireland for a few years and then on to Canada for my father's new job. A general recession in Europe in the late 50's combined with thousands of refugees escaping from the Hungarian Revolution, meant many emigrants were trying to make their way to the New World. Naval ships left over from the war were hastily turned into passenger boats. And vulnerable emigrants, desperate for new opportunities and security, believed all they read in brochures from shipping companies. Canada with its vast land and sparse population was far more welcoming and much easier to get into, than the US with its stringent immigrant quotas in place. The Greek liner we were on, the Olympus, had been headed to the port of Montreal before all hell broke loose the night before. I thought about my father anxiously awaiting us in Montreal and wondered if he knew what had happened.

We learned that at the height of the storm in the middle of the night the captain had to order some of his crew out of the lifeboats at gunpoint. Enough of them were about to mutiny to save their own skins. The radios weren't working and crew members were desperately pumping water out of the holds. Flares were sent up all night long searching for someone to rescue us, but in that storm no one was coming. We had lost all communication so we were literally lost at sea. There were several thousand people on that ship, and like the Titanic that had also left from Ireland 50 years before, it seemed like we too were destined for our watery graves.

And then something truly miraculous happened later the next day, just after I returned to the cabin from my mini expedition. We heard the sound of the engines start up again, and later someone informed us that radio communication was restored and we had our bearings once again. We had literally been saved from the brink of death for all of us.

But back to my adventure trying to find my way to the kitchen. After much wandering, meeting only men in Greek caps and speaking a language that sounded like Greek to me I began to remember the way to the dining room.

When I finally reached that large bright room there were crew members trying to clean up the smashed dinnerware all over the floors. Swinging doors at one end led to the kitchen, and I made my way there. For obvious reasons it looked like very little food preparation was going on. In fact I saw a large woman with a white apron and kerchief knotted behind her head waving directions to several people who were cleaning up the mess on the kitchen floor. This cook had an enormous amount of metal in her mouth. Having never seen so much gold and silver I wondered why anyone would take jewelry and stick it on their teeth.

"I Maria. You?" she asked alternately pointing to her own voluminous chest and my little one. I told her my name and then launched into my little request: "I was wondering if I could trouble you for some oranges for my little sister so she doesn't get scurvy."

"Hm??" she asked obviously having no understanding whatsoever.

But she did take my hand and led me to a huge metal door in the wall. She turned an enormous handle and freezing air was released into the sweltering kitchen. I tensed, remembering the witch in the Hanzel and Gretel story. Oh, no, I thought, she's going to throw me into that fridge and lock the door. There was a virtual tug of war going on as Maria tried to pull me into the fridge - really just so I could tell her what I wanted - and I just as strongly pulled away. The floor was wet and slippery and it wasn't long before we both went down amidst our laughter, falling apples and all kinds of other debris. Eventually I was able to communicate I wanted oranges by picking up apples, and showing her carrots for the color orange. She was so thrilled that someone would actually ever want food again that she gave me a bag with far more than I could carry. When I got back to the bunk with my precious cargo, of course my sister took one look at it and proceeded to throw up all over again.

There's one last episode to this story I would like to share with you. The next afternoon the storm had abated enough so that the captain ordered a huge party to give thanks our lives had been spared. The kids were invited into one large room to watch a movie and have ice cream. My mother joined the adults in the dining room for a kind of tea dance. What was so remarkable about that event was that when photos were put up in many corridors around the ship my mother was in most of those pictures dancing with someone who looked remarkably like Elvis Presley. As an adult I asked her why she was in so many photos and she said it was because she and my father were expert dancers. That's why people ended up watching her and the equally good dancer, Elvis, as I called him. So having just saved my sister's life I now felt I had to save my parents' marriage. I had visions of my mother and Elvis walking right past my poor father, as they came down the gangplank arm and arm and went off together to Hollywood. But all was fine, Elvis was nowhere to be seen and the three of us had a tearful and emotional reunion with my dad on the docks at Montreal.

To this day I have never gone on a boat or ship unless I know the shore will be visible. My story had a happy ending - we weren't escaping from a war torn country, although thousands of Hungarians were killed at that time, and it is estimated 200,000 fled their country.

Many refugees continue to tragically die in leaky and overcrowded boats crossing hazardous waters all over the world, and then face extreme hardship when and even if they make it to land. Here is one mother's prayer for her daughter as the young woman got into a leaky boat in Libya headed for somewhere in Europe.

Go, my beautiful child, go
Away from this life that is *my* life.
There is nothing here for you.
This magical boat will
Bring you to happiness and learning and love.
Be saved, my child,
Saved from a husband you will not love
Saved from motherhood too soon, when you are but a child yourself.
Go, my beautiful child, go.
Be free and safe across the sea.
Go.

# Phoebe's Metamorphosis

Phoebe Lowell began her walk at precisely 11 am with her usual measured no nonsense stride. It was her custom to go some distance through Central Park, and then stop at various bookshops on the return trip to her Fifth Avenue home.

This particular Tuesday in the fall of 1904 was noticeably crisp but sunny with leaves falling about her everywhere. Phoebe barely noticed. Her thoughts were on Henry, her philandering husband, who had not been seen by her, or apparently any of the household staff, for nearly a week now. It wasn't uncommon for him to go "missing," choosing to spend his leisure time with one mistress or another, though it had never bothered Phoebe before. But for some reason she felt this time it was different. For one thing he usually came back after a night or two of carousing, but now with this long absence she wondered if he had taken a trip with his latest lady friend, or perhaps he had even set up house somewhere with her. That, Phoebe reasoned, was more likely as he didn't much enjoy travel. He had made that fact patently clear on the one trip they had taken together to the Continent early in their marriage. For more than twenty five years they had remained together for convenience only, having little to nothing in common. It suited them both just fine - he for business reasons and she for financial security - to remain together living separate lives in their large Manhattan mansion.

Today Phoebe found herself a little further from home than was her custom; in fact not terribly far from her husband's law offices, as it happened, on 110th Street. As she began to contemplate the return loop she took note of her surroundings. On the other side of the street there was a small shop with a Bookseller sign hanging on the doorframe. Since she had never checked out this particular establishment, she decided to stop in before heading home. When she looked through the window, she saw a tiny shop, but one that felt welcoming with a table in the corner laid out with books, magazines and an open box of chocolates. Hundreds of books, new and old, were tidily placed on all available spaces. A man sat behind the counter reading so intently he didn't seem to hear the bell tinkle when Phoebe entered.

"Excuse me," she interrupted him as she walked to the counter, "would you happen to have a copy of Aeschylus' play *Oresteia* by any chance?"
Phoebe had been trying to get her hands on this work for many months, but to no avail.
"Why, yes I believe we do, but the question is where it might be," he scratched his head with a slight gesture of embarrassment. And then to Phoebe's horror a tear slid down his face.
"I'm so sorry" he apologized, "but I have just lost my wife and she was the one who took care of managing our inventory."

Though startled by this show of emotion, Phoebe took a moment to tell him she was sorry for his loss when he interrupted by saying:
"Oh no, no she didn't die. No, I have lost her to another man. Anna moved out several weeks ago and I'm a little at sixes and sevens here without her. She is the love of my life, you see."

Phoebe didn't *actually* see, as romantic love was not something with which she had had firsthand experience. Marriage to Henry had been a business transaction made between interested parties. She had acquiesced to her parents, believing one husband was as good as another. She would have preferred never to have married, instead dedicating her life to the study of philosophy and literature. But her parents wouldn't agree, and not agreeing also meant cutting out any financial support. So Phoebe married Henry and continued to read and study on her own as if her very life depended on it. It was an enormous relief to her when Henry suggested, a few years into their marriage, that they should keep separate quarters. They saw each other now and then for household matters and for obligatory social engagements. There had been no children and now, at the age of 52, parenthood was no longer a possibility for Phoebe.

Recovering himself somewhat, the man in the shop turned to Phoebe and put out his hand to shake hers.

"My name is Evander Wilkins and if you could give me a few days I will undoubtedly find that play for you. Would you mind coming back?" He was tall and very thin with a receding hairline and full beard, badly in need of trimming.

Phoebe looked at him for a moment and then said "I've never met anyone named Evander before. How did you get the name of such an obscure Greek figure?"

Mr. Wilkins smiled and said "I have three brothers named Adonis, Atlas and Zeus. I think I was the lucky one in that lottery, don't you?"

Phoebe nodded, and then asked, "But your parents must have studied Greek mythology then?"

"Not at all," he replied, seeming to enjoy this interchange and forgetting his bad luck for the moment. "No, they wanted us to have lofty ideals in life and so they thought names such as these would help us make intelligent and practical choices."

"And did they?" asked Phoebe, now fully engaged in this conversation.

"Well my brothers have had varying degrees of success with family and careers. And I'm very happy with my life. Or at least I was until a few weeks ago."

Feeling emboldened to ask some more questions since Evander had opened himself up, Phoebe asked:

"Do you know anything about this man then? The one your wife ran off with?"

"Just that he's very rich, and from something Anna said a few weeks ago, he's much older than she. Well you could say the same for me as I'm nearly 20 years her senior, but at least I've always loved her. This man will toss her out as soon as he tires of her. Isn't that what they usually do?" he asked bitterly.

"I'm sure I've no idea," Phoebe retorted quickly. Though if she were to be completely truthful she had lots of ideas, including first-hand experience with this very topic. In fact, she wondered if Anna could possibly be Henry's latest. It seemed farfetched but not outside the realm of possibility. After all, his office is not that far from this bookstore, she reasoned to herself. And though Henry could not have been accused of being much of a reader, he may have made a trip over to this shop now and then to pick up a book or magazine for a particular case.

"Have you ever seen this man in question?" she asked rather innocently.

"No but I accidentally saw his name on a note once. That was a hard pill to swallow."

Oh my, thought Phoebe. Do I really want to know if it's Henry? And what would I say to this man if that were the case? So she let it go and without giving him her own name told Evander she'd be back next Tuesday.


A few days later Henry returned home in a storm of anger. And though she was aching to know what happened, she didn't ask him any questions. He seemed more peeved than usual, snapping at the staff for every little infraction he perceived they were making. He offered no explanation for his disappearance and Phoebe did not ask, but she couldn't deny curiosity was getting the better of her.

The next Tuesday when she made her way to the bookstore again she felt some trepidation, though she also felt more alive with anticipation as well. This time as she entered the little shop she could not have been more surprised. For there, standing near Evander was a very pretty red haired young woman. Could this be the beautiful Anna, wondered Phoebe? Evander saw her enter and immediately came out from behind the counter, his face shining with the happiness of a newlywed.

"Oh there you are. I had forgotten to ask your name! I'm so glad you returned as my wonderful wife *did* locate that play for you."

"Oh, why, how do you do Mrs. Wilkins?" Phoebe paused for effect gazing directly at Anna before adding. "By the way, my name is Pheobe Lowell. Mrs. *Henry* Lowell."

Both of the Wilkins went noticeably ashen at this pronouncement causing Anna to actually grab the counter for support.

"So it *was* Henry," Phoebe confirmed to herself without saying a word. Having lost all sentiment for her husband, she nevertheless did find herself feeling something for this couple's distress, though she wasn't sure yet what that "something" was.

But in the next moment Evander, remembering he had already confided in Phoebe and probably worried what she might say in front of Anna, announced:

"I'm so happy that my wife has returned after a few weeks of vacation with her parents."

"Oh, hush Evander," Anna burst in. "Why all the secrets now that I'm standing next to his wife for goodness sake! I'm sure you're aware of your husband's long absence. Henry", she seemed to spit out the name, "booted me out when I told him I was pregnant with his child. I know the two of you barely speak so you probably won't understand when I tell you I really felt something for him. Evander knows all this and I'm grateful he took me back, I truly am Evander." At this softening of her tone she sent a tender look towards her doting husband. "My husband has agreed to call the child his own since we were never blessed that way. I made a terrible mistake but Evander has forgiven me and the truly amazing thing is we will finally have a child. Thank goodness Henry has no interest in scandal, or children apparently. I trust that you, Mrs. Lowell, will choose to keep this quiet as well."

Phoebe was experiencing an odd wave of emotions and asked for a chair and a glass of water to try to sort through them. Strange as it seemed, her sympathies were with this beautiful young woman who had naively believed she could have had a life with someone as well known and rich as Henry. And then Phoebe thought about Evander, who was apparently willing to take this woman and her baby back despite his own tremendous loss of pride and trust. And finally she felt something that she could only describe as a strange connection to the child now growing inside this woman. In that instant Phoebe made a life changing decision.

"Right," she said, rising from her chair with a determination and sense of purpose she had not felt in many years. "Here's what's going to happen, if you both agree. I want to make sure that this child gets every advantage and that means a comfortable life and a good education. I'll come back in

51

about a month and make a proposal to you. I don't know yet what that will be but I hope you will listen."

"Now wait a minute," Evander blustered, "I may not have the wealth and power of you uptown nabobs but I can sure take care of my own family very well thank you."

"Hold on, Evander," broke in Anna, "let's just see what Mrs. Lowell has to say first." And turning to the older woman she put her pretty little hand in Phoebe's, and with a beautiful smile and gentle lowering of her head so that her wavy red hair fell pleasingly over her face, she said, "Thank you for your concern, Mrs. Lowell. We both look forward to meeting with you again in several weeks, then." Though Phoebe protested, Anna would accept no payment for the Greek play which she carefully wrapped in newspaper before handing it over to Phoebe.

Back at home and with a new sense of purpose, Phoebe began an earnest investigation into her own finances. She knew the only way she could make any significant money without her husband's signature on every document was to privately sell her most precious jewels. So, with the help of a jeweler she located through discreet inquiries, she made enough money for her purposes from the sale of much of her expensive jewelry collection. Just as Henry never really noticed her, Phoebe reasoned, he was highly unlikely to observe her wearing a cheap replacement pastiche. Of course other women *would* notice, but Phoebe figured the few expensive pieces she had held on to would keep the hounds at bay. And, if she needed more capital she had that odd canvas her father had left her by that new European artist, with the strange name of Picasso. No doubt she could sell it to the Guggenheims if she had to.

Her next step was to find a banker who knew about building investments, but that she thought might be harder to do without it getting back to her husband. And then she recalled a distant cousin of hers who had done well for himself in banking. Anna sat down and composed a letter asking if he would be willing to meet with her the next week at a discreet location on a private financial matter. He replied back promptly and the meeting was set.

The proposal Phoebe made to the Wilkins some weeks later was fairly simple. With the help of her banker cousin she had found a three story building for sale on West 97th Street. That building, after Phoebe's planned renovations, would house the bookstore, an adjacent coffee shop the Wilkins would oversee, and upstairs the family would live in a comfortable two story flat. On the other side of the building the upper two stories would consist of rental apartments also to be managed by the Wilkins. After expenses, all earned revenue would go into a trust for the child's future. In turn the child would live with the Wilkins but would spend a lot of time with "Aunt" Phoebe who would influence all decisions about education and upbringing.

Anna, whose pregnancy was just starting to show, was absolutely thrilled with this arrangement. Evander, though, not as much as he believed he could give the child all that it needed in life. But with Anna's cajoling and his willingness to give her anything she wanted, he finally relented.

Renovation of the new building could not begin until March and that was also the month Anna's baby was due. Over the winter months Phoebe found herself drawn to Anna for her exceptional beauty and surprising business acumen, and to Evander for his quick mind and for their shared love of learning. The threesome became closer as they made plans for the

53

child and the various businesses the couple would run.    Phoebe found herself smiling more, losing patience with people less, and even tolerating Henry to a degree she hadn't experienced in years.

On March 25, 1905 a beautiful little girl came into the world.  Though her mother didn't love the name, Evander and Phoebe prevailed and called her Athena Persephone Wilkins.  Athena grew up to be a beautiful red haired young woman much like her mother, and loving and curious like the only father she had ever known.   But most of all she was bright, proud and fiercely independent, exactly as her adored Aunt Phoebe wanted her to be.

## Divorce in the time of Covid-19

Aviva looked over to Josh, her husband of 10 years, and sighed. The TV was tuned to CNN with the same "virus" news blasting away. Was there any aspect of the pandemic not covered yet she wondered? Josh had been building a new Lego structure with their son Adam much of the afternoon. Now he was stretched out in his favorite armchair taking a nap, while nearby the children were fighting over the iPads. Nine year old Rachel was using the slightly more up to date version so of course 5 year old Adam wanted hers. How could Josh sleep through all of this fighting, Aviva wondered, while she sorted another load of laundry and started to think about their next meal. Maybe we'll order take out tonight, she thought, as another round of mac and cheese couldn't be healthy for the kids.

Aviva had not been happy for some years and had been preparing to file for divorce. But now they had been ordered to "shelter in place" because of the pandemic, and all normal business was put on hold. Several weeks before the order came down from the Governor, Aviva had tried to start the process with her own attorney, though she hadn't talked to her husband about it. She knew without a doubt that he would attempt to talk her out of it. Now she couldn't do much about getting the process moving at all, as her lawyer wasn't answering her emails.

For the last couple of years Aviva and Josh had gone to therapists, both family and individual, to try to resolve their differences. The truth was that they were very different people trying to make their family work. Aviva knew Josh still loved her and wanted to save their marriage, for the sake of the children if for nothing else, but frankly she was bored with what the marriage offered her. She had a rewarding career as a children's book illustrator while her husband worked in an architectural firm. He plodded along in his comfort zone designing apartment buildings and banks, boring by Aviva's estimation, but nevertheless she had to admit it did pay the bills.

Now being around Josh day after day was wearing her down, though the schedule they had worked out kept them apart most of the time. Each was able to do their respective jobs every day, and also do home schooling with Rachel, games with Adam and plenty of computer face time with friends and extended family for themselves. Every day one of them would go for a bike ride or neighborhood walk with the kids, but almost never all four of them together. That was "me time" for the one left at home. Nights after the children went to bed, Aviva generally watched a movie while Josh did whatever he did on the computer, Aviva didn't ask him. It was generally working as Josh gave her the space she needed, but still did his share with the children for the most part. With their housekeeper now, of course, staying in her own home, Aviva gladly did most of the work around the house with a little help now and then from Josh or Rachel, as she liked the physical exercise it provided. She found herself busy from sunup to bedtime every day, with little time to brood over the divorce she had wanted to initiate.

Now she noticed, as she loaded the laundry back into the basket to be distributed to various drawers and closets, that things had finally quieted down in the family room. Adam had rolled away from Rachel and was lying on his side, uncharacteristically still. Rachel was happily oblivious now that her brother had left her alone. Aviva put the basket down and went over to Adam. His cheeks were very flushed. A sinking feeling went through her entire body when she saw him cough with difficulty. He had been coughing over the last few days, but she didn't think much of it as he always got allergies every spring, and he had seemed as energetic as usual.

"Oh my God, no." she wailed as she violently shook Josh. "Josh, Josh wake up. We have to get Adam to a doctor right now!"

Josh didn't wake up easily, but somehow he heard the panic in Aviva's voice, jumped out of the chair instantly and went over to Adam. In the meantime Aviva grabbed Rachel and took her and the iPad upstairs to her daughter's room.

"Stay here, Rachel, until we can get Adam looked after."

"Does he have it Mom? Will I get it too?" she asked with utter fear expressed in her entire face.

"We don't know yet but it's probably just a cough," she told her daughter with no conviction in her voice at all. "Can you stay here and entertain yourself for a bit until we take care of things with Adam?"

Aviva ran downstairs and asked Josh if he'd called the medical number they had up on the fridge. He said he wanted to take Adam's temperature first so he could give them accurate information. Aviva hadn't even thought of that; her impulsiveness led to complete panic and she would have been unable to answer any of their inevitable questions. She also knew tests for the virus were few and far between so they might not even know if he was infected. And what about Rachel and the rest of them, she wondered. For now she focused all her attention on Adam. Josh looked worried as he glanced at the thermometer and announced quietly so only Aviva could hear. "Not good, it's 103 right now." He picked up the phone while Aviva put on one of the two pairs of clean surgical gloves, and the last mask they had left.

57

She went over to Adam and tried to hold him but he just took one look at her and started to wail. "It's okay sweetie. Remember how we saw all those people wearing masks on the TV? It's really okay and will keep everyone feeling better. You don't want your sister to get sick, too, do you Sweetie?"

"Yes," he sobbed, "She wouldn't give me her iPad." And then his whole body was wracked with another violent cough.

Josh was off the phone now and he told her they were going to send an ambulance.

"They also said one parent could go with him in the ambulance as long as no one else was sick in the house. I'll go. You stay here with Rachel."

"Shouldn't I go?" asked Aviva. "He'll probably ask for me."

"No, you're better with Rachel than I am, and I'll be able to ask all the right questions."

Aviva bristled a bit but knew that what Josh was saying was true. "Here", she said without arguing further. "Take my mask and gloves or they won't let you in at all, and call me as soon as you can."

It took nearly three excruciating hours for Josh to call and tell her they had admitted Adam with a most likely confirmed case of Covid-19. They were just about to take an X-ray of his lungs. He said they had put Adam into a special pediatric section of the hospital, set up only for kids with the virus. For the time being they were letting him stay with his son on the chair near the bed, but he was not allowed to touch Adam who kept reaching his arms up to Josh to pick him up. All of this was heartbreaking for Aviva to hear.

But with that amazing resilience children often exhibit, within a few days Adam was feeling much better. Though Josh did tell her sadly a baby and a

12 year old had died in the same ward. Josh had barely left Adam's side for three days, not allowing her to come in his stead.

"No point in infecting the whole family is there?" he told her in one of their conversations. "You stay with Rachel. They'll probably release him by tomorrow. He's doing so much better and frankly they need the bed."

Aviva did hear back from the lawyer during the time Adam and Josh were at the hospital. She halfheartedly answered his questions and promised to send along the paperwork as soon as she could. But she spent her days worrying about someone else in the family getting the virus next, and Adam not fully recovering. She even started to think more positively about Josh, how he was really a great dad, and about the happy days earlier in their marriage.

As it turned out she never did get around to filling out those forms. Because within a week after Adam had come home, once again a healthy and happy 5 year old, Josh himself was admitted to the hospital. And suddenly Aviva found herself crying day and night for his recovery. She started pleading with God to save him and she would do whatever God wanted her to. She'd be a model wife and wouldn't complain about anything ever again, she promised. She knew now that Josh had discouraged her from going to the hospital so as to lessen her exposure and, in so doing, had increased his own risk for the sake of their child.

It was now a few days after Josh had been admitted but he was unable to speak to her. He had been put on a ventilator somehow he was sharing with another patient. How did that work, she wondered? Do they now get half the air they need? There was no one she could ask that question to, as of course she wasn't allowed into the hospital. The last thing the family needed was for her to come down with the virus too. So she texted him daily telling him to please get well and that she loved him. He was too sick to answer, and the health care staff were too frazzled to keep her informed. One day she got a call from Josh's older sister, Carol, who was sobbing uncontrollably. "Josh told me a few months ago that he thought you might file for divorce. Why, Aviva? He loved only you and you know, you broke his heart. I don't think he has much will to live, if you want to know what I think." Carol's words hit Aviva particularly hard as things had changed completely for Aviva now. Yes, she probably would have proceeded with the divorce if times had been normal. But now she started to wonder if maybe she should have worked harder at making their marriage work, instead of always being so ready to find Josh's shortcomings.

And now all was lost because Josh died a week after he was admitted, alone with no family members by his side. At his virtual memorial service sometime later, Aviva ended the eulogy with the following: "I am heartbroken at the loss of my husband. I wish I had appreciated Josh more when he was alive, and most important that I had told him so. He was really a good man and a wonderful father who loved his family with all his heart.

"Try to imagine what life would be like without that someone who is part of your life now. Thousands of people across the globe are facing this new reality of living without those people they love because of this cruel pandemic. It's too late for me but I implore you to show your love to those closest to you, and above all tell them how much they mean to you. You might never get a second chance."

# Covid-19 in a Brooklyn Apartment Building

## Ben and Naomi

**April 2022**

Darrell raised the foot of the recliner and prepared to entertain his three grandchildren for the next couple of hours while their mother did some errands. Over the last two years he had told them many stories about what had happened in his building during the pandemic, but they never seemed to get tired of his storytelling.

Darrell thought of this building as his own, as he had lived in it for more than 40 years. He and his wife Erma had come as "immigrants" to New York from Louisiana back in the 80s. A few years later they had a daughter, the children's mother, whom they named Louisa after the state they had left. He spent most of those early years working as the Maintenance Supervisor at various hotels in Manhattan. Over the years, he had built a friendly relationship with Mrs. Gupta, the owner and resident of the largest unit on the fifth floor. One day she offered the family a larger apartment on the first floor, free rent and a generous wage to do what he had been doing all of his career. And so with that, Darrell became the Super of his own building.

Now he reveled in the loving attention given him by his grandkids as they gathered around his chair. Especially since Erma had passed away from a recurring bout of cancer four years before. It was a rare day when Darrell didn't wake up with a raw empty feeling from missing her familiar presence. So it was a comfort that he had his daughter and grandkids nearby, and his busy and satisfying job.

61

"Granddad," asked five year old Letitia. "Tell us that story again about 404. I like that one. It's sad." The children had picked up their grandfather's habit of identifying tenants by their apartment number, though it always sounded comical to Darrell coming from a child.

At the time of Covid-19, Mrs. Judith Levine lived in 404. She was well into her 80s but loved her independence, refused to move into one of her children's homes, or God forbid, into Assisted Living. But during the worst of the pandemic, her son Nate insisted he pick her up and bring her to his home in Connecticut. She fought him tooth and nail but lost that battle in the end. Passover began on a Wednesday night, and sure enough early that morning Nate came to get her. Darrell still remembers her sad wave goodbye through the passenger window of the car. That was the last time he was ever to see her.

"And then what happened? I forget," Letitia asked.
"A little later that same day my doorbell rang and a guy said he was from a food delivery service," Darrell reminded the children.
"I have a big pre-paid Passover food order for 404 but they're not answering. Can I leave it with you?" he had asked.
"Now what was I going to do with a box full of Passover food like gefilte fish and matzo ball soup meant for Mrs. Levine?"
"Eat it?" asked Leticia.
"No way. I had my Easter ham waiting on the counter and I didn't think it would be right to mix kosher food with my ham."
"So what'd you do?" asked Darnell, the rambunctious 8 year old who was named for his grandfather, Darrell. His nickname "Darn" stuck, as someone didn't get the spelling quite right on his birth certificate.

"Well I did the only right thing I could think of since Mrs. Levine didn't believe in cell phones so I couldn't call her. I took it up to 321, the Goldman's. They're that very religious family with probably 10 kids. One of them told me once they get "a new one" every year. I called Mrs. Goldman and told her I would leave the box on her doorstep and that she could thank Mrs. Levine when she saw her next. But that never happened. Mrs. Levine got the virus and passed away in a hospital near her son's home."

"Will we get it too, Granddad?" asked Letitia in a scared voice..

"No way Honey. That dratted awful thing is finally gone from Brooklyn, and everywhere else, so you guys are safe now."


"But there's another story I never told you kids yet." He called out to his smart and beautiful 14 year old granddaughter, Nia, whom he once told not to be too sad that he probably wouldn't be around when she became the first ever African American Woman President!

"Nia, open up that cabinet over there where you'll find Ben's story. He gave me a copy after he wrote it. Go ahead and read it for us."

# Ben's Story

My name is Ben and I live in a two bedroom apartment in Brooklyn. It's a fine five story building with a diverse group of tenants whom I rarely, if ever, see. That's because I'm the General Manager of the Koch Theater. You may have even seen one of the more famous musicals or plays performed there over the years. Anyway, my job meant that I worked most nights when the theater was in operation and then slept into the early afternoon next day. So I didn't really get to see or meet any of my neighbors, except occasionally at the mailboxes.

Of course that all changed in March of this year when NYC basically closed down everything. My contract meant I continued to be paid, but I had to make the most heart-wrenching decisions to furlough most of our employees. When eventually we could bring some of them back this past summer I had already lost a number of my best people to the virus. But that's a story for another day.

So there I was stuck in my apartment, like much of the planet's population, unable to do much of anything. Like everyone else I connected with old friends from college, facetimed with my nieces, and of course kept in touch with my parents who lived in New Jersey.

Conversations from my side went something like this:

"Are you staying indoors Mom?" "Dad, did you get that garden planted yet?"

Conversations from my Mom were invariably on her favorite topic: "Ben, you're already 42. This would be the perfect time to find a wife online.

With this kind of time on your hands now, you could have been married and divorced three times already!"

I knew she was right about having the time but I didn't mention the inertia I felt. The casual women I met at work never seemed to lead to a meaningful relationship. Up until now it had all seemed okay. But now, frankly, staying in my apartment day after day with only Chester the Cat to talk to was getting really old. And added to this was the fact that for Passover I was programmed to join my family's Zoom Seder. That, I was not really looking forward to. My parents and my brother's family feeling sorry for me eating a solo meal in my solo apartment.

The seder came and went and it was somewhat of an ordeal as my mother couldn't resist asking me every few minutes "if that was all I was eating". I must say my mouth did water when I saw the feast each family had on their laden tables while I had ordered takeout matzo ball soup and a little piece of chicken for my meal. At about 10 o'clock the kids started fighting over finding the Afikomen. That's the piece of matzo that's hidden and must be redeemed with a hefty payment from the parents to keep their offspring from losing it completely for the rest of the seder. That's when I announced that I would be signing off as I was getting very tired. "Why?" asked my mother, "have you had a particularly busy day?"
"Ok, Goodnight everyone." And then for good measure I added, "Stay safe" which had become the mantra for everyone, especially those of us living at the epicenter.

I didn't immediately head off to bed, but decided to go out to the front of the building first. The air now was actually almost clean, the streets eerily quiet, and wonder of wonders, I could see the beautiful full moon more clearly than ever before. I hadn't been outside for very long when I heard the front door open behind me. There standing at the top of the step was a slim young woman with the most amazing red hair. She looked like the perfect person to play Little Orphan Annie, though of course much too old for the part. I called out "Hello" to her as she stopped near the door far enough away from me to be considered acceptable. Did someone with a macabre sense of humor pick six feet as the obligatory distance for both above and below ground?

"Hi," she answered. "Nice evening. Do you live in the building?"
"Yes in 512. I just came out to get some air after 3 hours at a virtual seder with my family."
She laughed and then added, "I had a wonderful seder with my neighbors."
"How did you manage that?" I asked, and with a little malice in my voice that she had escaped my particular fate.
"Well, there are five Jewish families on my floor, it's the fourth floor. One of them, though, is Mrs. Levine who took off with her son this morning. Anyway we all decided we would leave our apartment doors open, and when one person started a song during the seder, no matter where we all were in our own seders, we would join in. We planned it so that we would all eat at the same time, come to each of our doors and "verbally" share with the others what was on our menu. We even invited our non-Jewish neighbors, who were interested, to leave their doors open so they could listen in if they wanted to. It worked so well that in fact we're going to do it all over again tomorrow night for the Second Seder."
"That sounds amazing and so much more meaningful than trying to do a virtual seder." I said. "By the way I'm Ben,"
"And I'm Naomi", she answered.

We covered many topics on the steps that night, always properly socially distanced. I learned she played 2nd violin for the Metropolitan Orchestra, which was also of course furloughed, but that she nevertheless practiced for hours every day. That she was 38 and had never married, and that she loved her many nieces and nephews.

I loved my nieces too, but maybe not so much through a computer when they were fighting!

"Well, I better get inside," Naomi said after several hours of our talking on the steps. "It's starting to get a bit chilly. Hey Ben? Would you like to share my Seder table tomorrow night? I haven't been out for weeks, not even to get food as I have everything delivered. And I have no symptoms. What about you?"

"Yep, same story for me. Other than a daily bike ride I rarely go out, and I also get everything delivered."

"Okay shall we say 7 pm tomorrow night? I'm in apartment 413. And you don't need to bring anything as I have more than enough for two. Oh and by the way" she laughed "the doors will all be open again, just in case you get any improper ideas."

I am writing this on October 16, 2020 a full 6 months after Naomi and I met on the steps of our building on Passover during Covid-19. Can I tell you how I am the happiest and luckiest man in New York as tomorrow is our wedding day? Even my mother has fallen head over heels for Naomi, and not just because her 42 year old son is finally getting married!

What can I say? There are no words to describe the loss and misery this pandemic caused to so many all over New York and the world. And it will be many years before we can get back to some semblance of normalcy, especially in this country. But had it not been for those awful dark days

Naomi and I would never have been granted this chance at love, happiness and the end to that terrible loneliness of having to shelter in place completely alone.

**April 2022**

"Wow," Nia sighed after she finished the story. "That was *so* romantic. What happened to them Granddad? Did they get married?"

"They sure did. I was there. Lots of people from the building were there too. Boy they have a lot of fun at those Jewish weddings with the bride and groom up on chairs. It was just like being in New Orleans during Mardi Gras."

"Anyway, guys. I have to get moving. Tonight is Passover again and I have a few things to do for the tenants. Let's go together."

Darrell first took the children up to the 5th floor where he had a delivery of flowers to make.

A young woman immediately answered Letitia's knock.

"Who is it, Honey?" came a man's voice from the kitchen.

"It's me. Darrell."

"Oh those are gorgeous! Thank you, Darrell," the young woman smiled as she took the bouquet. "Please, come in."

Just then the man came out of the kitchen holding a beautiful red-haired baby in his arms.

"Hi Guys. You must be the famous grandkids Darrell never stops telling us about. My name is Ben and this is my wife Naomi. And you can all have a turn holding little Rachel as long as you don't fight over her."

"And," added Naomi, "you all must have some of the chocolate cake I made especially for Passover. You have just given Ben the greatest excuse *not* to save it for dessert tonight!"

# Covid-19 in Brooklyn Apartment Building

## Emmie and Thea

Emelda, or Emmie as everyone called her, collapsed her umbrella as she entered the building in Brooklyn where her employer, Thea Kazan, had lived for many years. Emmie had been her caregiver for the last six years, working the day shift Mondays to Fridays. Although Miss Kazan was wheelchair-bound, she was never a burden for Emmie as she had come to love her kind and considerate employer.

Today's routine was no different from most other days in Emmie's life, except that Covid-19 had attacked NYC with a vengeance. She donned her gloves and mask before going into Miss Kazan's apartment on the building's first floor. Emmie had pretty much worn that same mask every day for more than two weeks now, as masks were like gold and all you could do if you had one was wash it and hope it held up for a few more days.

Although Emmie had to leave her baby son Ernesto and 5 year old daughter Sonia with her sister Maria every day to come to work, she nevertheless felt blessed that she had a job, unlike millions of people across the country. Maria had been working as a housekeeper at a nearby Marriott, but that job had evaporated months ago. The two young women already shared an apartment, so it fell on Maria to care for Emmie's children every day while Emmie was at work. But as soon as her sister got home, Maria would immediately leave. Emmie suspected she was going to her new boyfriend's apartment, but she never asked and just hoped Rodolfo didn't come to their flat while she was at work.

"I've got to get out of here, Emmie. I can't take kids and this small space any longer."

"Don't be back too late, Maria. You know I've got to catch the 8:20 bus to Miss Kazan's tomorrow morning."

Thea Kazan was 83 and had never married. She had come to New York in her mid 20s after an American man of Greek descent she met in an Athens bar promised her a "wonderful" life in New York. He had even given her a shiny engagement ring to seal the deal. So she followed him to the U.S. only to discover he already had a wife, and was hoping to set up Thea as his "special lady friend." She forever cursed her stupidity at not even having that worthless ring evaluated before leaving Athens.

"I will never be anyone's mistress, you worthless piece of trash," Thea angrily shouted at him as she left the restaurant where he had just told her they couldn't get married for a while, well actually not until he left his wife. That was the last she ever saw of him.

Thea had arrived in New York on a three month's visitor visa, but took a chance and stayed on illegally as she had come to love the vitality of the city. Her first job was as a waitress in a Greek restaurant. And she also tutored the children of some of the church members at a local Greek Orthodox church. After spending many years and hundreds of dollars on lawyers, she was finally able to get a green card and then her U.S. citizenship. Things were a lot easier for immigrants those days than in the current climate, she knew. Later she legally brought her much younger brother Nikos to New York. It didn't take Nikos long to land a good job in a printing company. Unfortunately, there he met his loud and obnoxious wife, Denise. Try as she might, Thea could never warm up to Denise, though she was very close to their only child, Melinda. In spite of her

71

mother, Melinda had turned into a lovely young woman and was now studying marketing at NYU. Thea, herself, had worked hard to get her teaching diploma and had had a satisfying career as a teacher in a local elementary school. She never married and had lived in this same apartment in Brooklyn for more than 30 years.

On this particularly wet Monday morning in April, Emmie warmly greeted Darrell, the building Super as she came into the lobby and he was just leaving. When she first started working for Miss Kazan, Emmie made sure to introduce herself to Darrell. It proved to have been a wise move as they had developed a friendly acquaintanceship, and genuinely liked each other. Over the years Emmie had called on Darrell more than a few times to help with a blocked drain or a switch that didn't work right, and she always found him to be kind, responsive and helpful.

And now Emmie quietly let herself into Thea's apartment as she knew that sweet lady would most likely still be asleep. After hanging up her coat and washing her hands thoroughly, Emmie began to get Thea's light breakfast going. Besides Emmie, there was always an evening person, working through an agency, who was there from the time Emmie left until 11 pm. This arrangement had been working out fine as Thea usually slept until after Emmie arrived, but recently Emmie had begun to wonder if Thea might need overnight help as well.

Carrying tea and a toasted bagel, Emmie went into the dark bedroom and immediately heard labored breathing and wheezing coming from the bed. She put the tray down and went over for a closer look. Thea appeared to be asleep but her face was so flushed that alarm bells began to ring for Emmie. Making sure her mask was completely covering her nose and

72

mouth and her gloves were on tight, she slipped a thermometer under Thea's tongue.

"Please, don't let it be the virus," Emmie prayed. Thea's temperature was registering at 101 and she still had her eyes shut.

"I better call Nikos and ask him what I should do," she decided, with trepidation that somehow Denise would blame her for bringing the virus in from the outside. It wouldn't be the first time that woman had found fault with one thing or another. It seemed obvious to Emmie that she was jealous of the relationship Emmie and Thea had developed over the years, and so took her vengeance out on Emmie at every opportunity.

"We'll drive over right away, Emmie," Nikos told her after she reached him in his apartment in Queens. "There's so little traffic it won't take very long. In the meantime, please call her doctor and find out what you should do."

Emmie had been hearing how the hospitals were so overwhelmed they had opened up emergency facilities like that huge hospital ship treating patients with the virus. She finally reached the doctor just before Nikos and Denise arrived, both wearing plexiglass shields, masks and gloves. The doctor said that they'd be sending an ambulance but it could take some time as all the drivers were completely overwhelmed. The thought of spending the next several hours with Denise in the apartment was too much for Emmie, so she said she would go to the drug store for a few things as long as they were there to watch over Thea.

"When you get back you can make us some sandwiches for our lunch!" Denise yelled rudely at the closing front door.

"Nikos, stay out of your sister's room you stupid man. I don't want to get this virus from you next!"

It took about an hour for Emmie to get in and out of Walgreens, though looking for hand sanitizer was of course an exercise in futility. The rain had stopped so she walked around the neighborhood for a while to kill time. When she returned, the apartment was already empty.

Emmie started to really worry now for Thea's health, but also something else was causing her tremendous anxiety. Today was payday for her last two weeks of work. Her rent was due the next day and her landlord was hounding all the tenants and telling them they had to pay or be out on the streets. She knew what he was threatening was illegal as they were supposed to be protected from this kind of action, but her status as an undocumented worker put her and her entire family in jeopardy, and he knew it.

Years earlier Thea had asked Emmie to have Darrell put a lock on one of the drawers so they could keep cash handy in that drawer, and also keep it safe from the many agency women coming in and out every day. Since Emmie preferred to be paid in cash there was usually a fairly substantial amount kept in that drawer. However, today when she went to open it to take out the exact amount she was owed, she noticed the lock was already open and all the money gone. Emmie remembered she had unlocked it when she first arrived, but then the kettle started to whistle so instead she ran into the kitchen to turn it off. With Thea's blessing she had been taking her own pay for years. Denise must have taken the money, maybe while Nikos was with his sister. Now what do I do? Emmie asked herself. In a panic for many reasons, one of which was being accused of stealing the money herself, she went next door to Darrell's to ask his advice.

"I guess you were out, Emmie, when the ambulance came to get her. She looked very poorly when they took her away," Darrell informed her.

"Oh poor Miss Kazan. I hope she'll be okay," sobbed Emmie. And then Emmie told Darrell about the missing money.

"I don't have any savings at all to get us through until Miss Kazan gets back. Where am I going to find $1000 for the rent tomorrow? That witch of a woman is sure to get me arrested. What will happen to my kids if I get deported?" Emmie sobbed.

At that very moment the "witch" and her husband were coming back into the building since they couldn't go to the hospital with Thea. When Denise saw Emmie, she started a tirade loud enough for the tenants on the next floor to hear.

"First you bring that virus into this building and infect Thea. Then you steal all the money in her drawer, you wicked girl. I'm calling the police on you."

"Hold on, hold on, Denise." Nikos tried to calm his out-of-control wife to no avail. "How do you know money was stolen? Let's not get ahead of ourselves here. Emmie, do you know what Denise is talking about?"

"Well I happen to know there was more than $2000 in that drawer," shouted Denise before Emmie could say a word.

"And how would you know that, Mrs. Kazan, unless you were in that drawer counting the money." Darrell was really angry now.

"Why don't you ask *her* where the money is?" snarled Denise pointing to Emmie.

While she was momentarily distracted, Nikos grabbed the purse from Denise and started to look through it. Sure enough, there was a large wad of money stashed in the side pocket.

75

"How could you steal that money and then accuse an innocent woman? This is the last straw Denise. I've had it with you. We're done."

"Well, wait a minute, Honey. I was just taking what we'll get after she dies. We all know everyone old who gets this virus dies."

"I suggest you shut up, Denise," her husband warned her. "Emmie, I'm really sorry about this mess up. Please just take the money. We can sort out everything once Thea gets well and returns to us."

But sadly Thea did not get well. She died two days later of Covid-19. In her will she left her beloved niece Melinda and brother Nikos two thirds of her fairly substantial estate, and the other third went to Emmie. There was also a letter she had left for Darrell in which she requested that Emmie's family move into her own unit. After determining Emmie now had sufficient funds for this more expensive apartment, and knowing she was a reliable and honest person, Darrell gladly took care of the rental arrangements. He also put Emmie together with another elderly woman in the building needing additional daily assistance. This new job allowed her to be with her own children more, and to be a little less dependent on Maria's help.

As for Denise? Nikos divorced her as soon as he could make all the arrangements. But before the divorce settlement was finalized, as a final parting shot Nikos gave his third of Thea's estate to his daughter Melinda, so that Denise could never get her hands on his sister's money.

## Covid-19 Brooklyn Apartment Building

## Cheryl and Mario

Cheryl stripped off her protective coverings in the locker room of Maimonides Hospital, before she ventured out of the building. As a nurse in the ICU, she and her colleagues had been horrified at how strict protocols for protective gear had been relaxed due to massive shortages. Everyone in the country, including every politician, knew how these shameful shortages threatened the lives of so many health workers, but few seemed to be able to find a solution, even several months into the pandemic.

Cheryl could barely get herself up, once she sat down to remove the booties, as she'd been on her feet for more than 12 hours straight. And that was true for yesterday and the day before too. As a single woman with an apartment nearby in Brooklyn, it seemed her supervisor asked her to work more shifts than others. Cheryl knew the hospital wouldn't have to consider any extended family members for her. Or the incredible hazards health workers' families were daily exposed to. So far she had escaped any symptoms, but like every other exposed and essential worker in the country she didn't know how much longer her luck would hold out.

Two years ago Cheryl had jumped at the opportunity of moving up from North Carolina and taking a gig as a traveling nurse. The temporary job at Maimonides was supposed to last only six months, but she was so skilled and liked by everyone, that when she was offered a permanent position she gladly stayed. Except for the years when she went away to college for her RN degree, she had spent her entire happy young life on her parent's horse farm in a beautiful part of the state.

Cheryl rode her bike to and fro from work, feeling safer than on public transportation. That's illogical, she told herself. You're already surrounded by Covid patients all day long! But riding her bike was one way to enjoy the quiet and clear air outdoors after being cooped up for so many hours.

As she let herself into her building, she noticed a flyer just inside the front door advertising "a loving person to walk your dog" with a special discount for healthcare workers. She didn't really need the discount as her salary, plus the money her father insisted in regularly depositing into her checking account, was more than enough these days. What was there to spend it on anyway, she wondered, as she was so weary when she got home that she couldn't begin to think about ordering anything online.

"Oh you poor, poor Cora," she cooed to her golden Labrador who had now been cooped up for hours, since the neighbor's son had texted that he walked her around noon. One trip outside in 14 hours was not enough for her beloved Cora.

"Okay let's go out, and then I'll give you a nice dinner of dried food. Oh yum!" Actually, anything sounded yummy to Cheryl as her last meal had been hours ago when some kind restaurant owner had brought over several dozen large boxes of pizza for the workers in the ICU.

On the way out for their walk, Cheryl picked up a copy of the flyer and thought maybe she could have a real dog walker come several times a day. She didn't want to put Cora in a kennel, but she knew what she was doing to the poor dog now was nothing less than cruel. So while she was waiting for Cora to do her business, Cheryl called the number on the flyer.

"Hello, I understand you walk dogs, is that right?"

"Yes, that's quite true. My name is Mario and who am I speaking to please?" asked the man with a distinct accent she couldn't place right away.

"Well I might be looking for someone. Where are you located? If not too far from me and if you're free maybe we could meet on the street somewhere. I have my *pretty large* dog with me now." Just in case you're an axe murderer, Cheryl added to herself.

She had stopped to give Cora a chance to sniff at a post and gave Mario the address of the boarded up store near where she was standing.

"Will be there in 5 shakes," he told her.

Five shakes? Okay I guess it takes all kinds but hopefully he's not some weirdo guy, Cheryl wondered, hoping she hadn't made a big mistake in contacting him.

The man who rode up on his bike wore a strange red hat that was sitting on an angle on his head, reminding Cheryl of a European's chef's cap she'd seen in a book once. He got off his bike, and immediately bent down to greet Cora, who wagged the entire back half of her body in response! A little closer to me than the required six feet, Cheryl thought, but held back her comments.

Okay, fine, thought Cheryl, he wants me to know he likes dogs. Some protection *you* provide Cora! I'll need to get you trained better one of these days when I have a few extra hours in my day.

When he stood up and stepped back, she noticed he was slightly shorter than she and very thin, even wiry. He looked to be a few years older, though of course she couldn't tell for sure. He was not wearing a mask, which irritated her, but he had a warm and bright smile and seemed to give her his entire attention.

"So can you tell me what your qualifications are to be a dog walker?"

"Well I love dogs. And I need a job. What else is there to tell you?"

"How long have you been walking dogs?" she asked a little angry at his offhanded answer.

"Oh you would be my first customer. I lost my job as the chef at Vittali's last month."

"Vittali's, wow." She had only heard of the restaurant as it was way out of range for her and her friends. One day, she thought, I'll get there. First it has to open again and then I'll need a rich guy to take me!

"I am a good handy man so can do lots for you. Are you working all day and need someone for what's his name?"

"What's his name is Cora, and he's a she."

"Oh, well I can walk Cora a few times a day, do your shopping for what you need. You still have a job? That's great. Good for you. What do you do?"

"I'm a nurse at Maimonides."

"Oh," he said, taking a few more steps back and away from her.

"I hear you guys are getting the Covid more than everyone else. Every day I like to stand on the street and clap for you brave doctors and nurses. Tell you what, Miss..?"

"Cheryl."

"Okay Miss Cheryl why don't you give me a chance. I'll come three times a day to start. Can we say $75 a day which is a great discount!"

That seemed a little steep to Cheryl, but she was starting to appreciate his upbeat nature, even though he had recently lost an excellent job. She decided she would ask Darrell, the building Super, to watch what was going on for the first few weeks.

"So please you give me your address and your schedule, okay? Then I won't come on your days off, just when you're not there. Do you want my driver's license so that way you can do a check on me? They do that in my restaurant, well they used to when it was open. I am honest, didn't break any laws that I know of anyway ha ha." He had a habit of waving his arms wildly when he spoke. Definitely Italian, Cheryl thought, and probably harmless, though how would I know for sure? But when he gave her a warm smile and his eyes crinkled up in a nice way, Cheryl decided to take a chance on him.

"Okay Mario, let's give it a try. I'm working tomorrow from 6 am to 6 pm. I'll take her out before I go to work. You should come by about 10 in the morning, then maybe 2 in the afternoon and again about 5:30 so I don't have to take her out as soon as I get home. Ring the Super's doorbell and he'll let you in. If things go well, then we'll work out another arrangement so you don't have to rely on the Super every day."
She gave him the address and he waved as he rode off on his bike shouting "Okie dokie. See you tomorrow. Please don't get sick."
Cheryl thought how sad the world had become when the chef for such a famous restaurant was reduced to walking dogs to survive.

Things went well the first couple of weeks so Cheryl felt comfortable enough giving Mario a key, with a promise from Darrell that he would try to check up on him now and then.

On a Tuesday during the third week of their arrangement, Cheryl was particularly exhausted after a long day of work, though she had taken her temperature every hour and so far it seemed to be normal. She figured she'd walk Cora to a takeout in the neighborhood and buy a hamburger for herself and one for Cora, mostly out of guilt at being gone so much. But when she opened her apartment door, she held back for a moment when she sensed someone was there. Cora greeted her with a big wag so there couldn't be anything wrong, could there, she wondered?

"It's okay, Miss Cheryl. It's just me, Mario. Sorry I'm a bit late. Anyway, I take Cora now. Sorry for disturbing." The only chefs she'd ever seen were the ones who yelled at their staff nonstop on TV shows. Mario seemed anything but the yelling type and in fact was the exact opposite. He couldn't have things easy right now, but the few times they had talked by phone, he always asked about her and never once complained.

As she hung up her coat she noticed there was a strange but lovely smell coming from the kitchen.

"What's that smell, Mario?"

"Oh just something special I make for your dinner. You must be tired. I buy all the ingredients. It's a little present for you for saving the lives of all those sad people."

"Wow Mario, you didn't have to do that. That's very kind of you. Can I pay you back for the ingredients and your time?"

"Don't worry now, we'll make things good at the end of the week."

"So do you want to stay for dinner?" she asked him suddenly, surprising herself. "You can be in the living room and I'll eat in the kitchen so you don't have to worry about getting 'the Covid' from me. Then you can tell me what's on this amazing looking menu."

While Mario was walking Cora she had a quick shower, and for the first time in many weeks took some extra care in picking her clothes and applying her makeup.

When Mario returned and they had settled down in their respective rooms to eat a truly amazing and unusual ravioli dish, she asked him if he was unable to find any other work. He told her the entire staff at Vittali's had been temporarily let go, though the owner wasn't sure if he could hold on to reopen. Mario decided to give up his apartment as he didn't have a lot of savings, and had been invited to move in with a sous chef from the restaurant. That man's wife still had a job in high tech so they were getting by, but just barely. Mario said he felt good he could contribute a little now that he was earning $450 a week working for Cheryl 6 days a week.

The weeks went by and gradually Cheryl and Mario got into a comfortable pattern. She would leave for work, he would walk Cora, buy food and cook a meal for the two of them. She was starting to have strong feelings for Mario but she sensed he was still afraid of getting close to her. For her part she wanted to protect him from exposure as much as she could. So they carried on with this platonic arrangement for nearly 6 months, talking for hours over their dinners until Cheryl could no longer keep her eyes open. And then gradually New York began to open up, and people started to get some semblance of normalcy back in their lives.

One day he told her he had fallen in love with her, kissed her passionately, put an elegant antique ring that had belonged to his grandmother on her finger, and that was that. They drove together, with Cora of course, to North Carolina so her parents could meet Mario. It didn't take long for them to see how much he loved their only child, and realize what a kind and talented man he was. Having such an amazing chef around didn't hurt either. Vittali's never did reopen in New York, so Cheryl's dad offered to help by investing in one of the many empty restaurants now dotting the streets of downtown Durham. People soon started to venture out for meals to places like Mario's restaurant, aptly named "Cora's Italian Ristorante". It soon became the place to meet and enjoy a fabulous dinner.

Both Cheryl and Mario sometimes felt sad that they had left New York and her apartment they had come to love as a couple. But they had their own little cottage conveniently built on the ranch years ago for Cheryl's grandparents. And Cheryl soon went back to work, this time at Duke Hospital not far from their new restaurant. She worked only part time so she could spend time with their delightful new baby. Of course the doting grandparents couldn't get enough of their precious grandchild and provided all the babysitting Mario and Cheryl could possibly need. And then there was also the beloved Cora, plus those exciting horses, making her one of the happiest and best entertained little girls in the whole state.

They gave her the unique name of Coviny. When anyone asked, they always repeated the made up story that she was named after an elderly aunt of Mario's who lived in Florence, and who had miraculously survived the terrible pandemic of 2020.

# Covid-19 in a Brooklyn Apartment Building

## Mike, Jeff and Larry

Mike, Jeff and Larry were the Tom, Dick and Harry of their high school, as they were always together and thick as thieves. Though they chose different activities in school, each was always there to support the other, whether it was basketball as in Mike's case, theater for Jeff or football for Larry. When one of the trio had a game or was in a play, the other two were virtually unavailable to do anything else. No one, parents and teachers or even girlfriends, could quite understand this special bond they had. It was just known and widely accepted throughout the town of Oakridge Iowa's only high school.

Not many in the trios' graduating class of 2016 went on to college, as this small town was first and foremost a meat packing "company" town. It was expected that kids follow in their parents' footsteps and take a job at the plant when they graduated. Mike's dad and Jeff's parents had worked at the Oakridge plant all of their kids' growing up years. Larry's parents ran a small grocery store where he spent many years helping out in some age appropriate way. And so when the boys graduated and each chose a different path from the expected one, there was shock and surprise expressed by family members and friends.

"What do you mean you're going to pursue a career in theater?" asked Jeff's father. "You don't really expect to live on that for the rest of your life, do you? Really??"
"I'd like to give it a try, Dad. Start small, doing box office and ushering work in Des Moines."

"And what do your buddies say, huh?" asked Jeff's dad as he shook his head in a show of incredulity that his own son would choose a path different from the one he himself had taken.

"Well, they're coming with me. I was going to tell you we have an apartment already. We used our savings for the first month's rent and Larry's parents were the co-signers on it. Mike already got a job in a senior home, doing cleanup and general work around the place. It's entry level but he wants to get his nursing degree and this will let him study part time."

"What do you mean he wants to be a nurse? That's not men's work. Is he gay or something? Don't tell me *you're* gay, Jeff!"

"No Dad we're not gay. We just want to try something different from staying here and working at the plant. If it doesn't work out we'll probably come back. C'mon Dad, it's not like we're going to New York! We'll only be sixty miles away!"

But, in fact, three years later, with some money and experience under their belts they did exactly that, and decided to try their hand at life in the Big Apple. Jeff landed the first job, working on stage lighting for the Schubert Theatre on Broadway. His hard work, can-do attitude and general friendliness had helped him move up rapidly at the theater in Des Moines, and gave him the advantage he needed to get the job in New York. Mike earned his LVN degree in Des Moines, and transferred to a nursing home in Brooklyn that was part of the same chain where he worked. Jobs came hardest to Larry who had been a busboy at several restaurants, but now with this move to New York, he said, he was going to try for a job as a waiter.

So in the summer of 2019 they packed their bags, said goodbye to various family and friends, including a few semi serious girlfriends, and headed off to NYC. Finding an apartment they could afford was going to be the

86

hardest part as rents were astronomical by any standards, especially for people coming from a rural state like Iowa! They knew it would have to be soon, though, as their hotel bill was eating up a chunk of savings.

Late on a Friday afternoon, just when they were getting pretty depressed about their prospects of ever finding affordable housing, Jeff saw a sign outside an apartment building in Brooklyn that looked promising.

The Super who showed them around introduced himself as Darrell. He asked if two of them would be sharing a room. Darrell didn't want problems right from the start leading to one or another moving out. Jeff said they had a plan for how to work out the arrangements. One person would sleep on the couch in the living room.

"But just to make sure it's all fair," Jeff explained. "We'll be rotating so you'd only have to sleep in the living room every third week!" Darrell thought that was quite creative and showed a strong connection between the guys. He liked this trio of young men, and so made the recommendation to the rental agent. Once the appropriate papers and deposit were accepted, they were able to move into their new home.

The friends soon settled into a routine, working hard at their various jobs. Larry eventually lined up another busboy job. He just couldn't convince a potential employer that he had the goods to be a waiter. As they had done in Des Moines, they worked out a fair arrangement where each paid according to his earnings level. That meant that Jeff paid the most, followed closely by Mike, and lastly Larry who additionally took care of shopping and some of the cooking to make up his part of the deal. They had even come up with a mutually accepted plan when someone wanted to bring a girl to the apartment. The simple rule was that if it was your week on the living room couch you couldn't bring a girl home for the night. Only "bedroom" guests were allowed!

Life was great, work was generally rewarding, and living in New York was truly exciting for these three rural young men. That is, until March 2020. That's when Covid-19 hit the country with a vengeance, and life as we knew it was never to be the same again.

By April, Mike's demeanor had changed overnight, when the senior home he worked at lost two residents and an employee to the pandemic in just one week. The hospitals in the City were overrun and people were dying by the thousands. Protective equipment, including masks, were few and far between for all healthcare workers, but especially for those in senior centers. So Mike came home every day and shuttered himself in his room to protect his roommates. The room rotation plan fell by the wayside through those awful weeks and months of the pandemic.

Jeff's theater closed in March and he lost his job. He hadn't even been there long enough to earn any benefits. Larry's restaurant also closed and he, too, had no salary protection. The landlord was forced to allow the renters, due to some official mayoral proclamation, to lapse on their rent but it would eventually have to be paid. Mike was working as many hours as he could. Gone was the jovial friend they had counted on to make them laugh.

One day in early May, Jeff got a call from his dad that his mom was seriously ill with the virus. His dad told him there were hundreds of positive cases at the Oakridge plant, but they were told they would have to work or lose their jobs. So his mom continued on until she couldn't work anymore. She was eventually sent to the ICU in Des Moines where, of course, no family members could see her.

"At least you're not forced to work there in New York like we are." Jeff had never heard such despair and bitterness in his dad's voice.

"Please don't go into work, Dad, even if you think you'll lose your job. I'll take care of you when I can work again."

"I have to work, Jeff. I haven't tested positive. Yet anyway. And Jeff, don't even *think* about getting on a plane to come home. You can't see Mom anyway. Your little sister is getting to be a really good cook, so we're okay." His voice caught in his throat as he said he couldn't see Jeff's mom or even talk to her as she'd been put on a ventilator.

These were very dark days for the trio. Jeff had never felt such despair and blamed himself for moving to New York and bringing his buddies with him. Just when they thought the news couldn't get any worse, they heard that Mike's dad tested positive. The boys spent their days worrying about getting the virus, missing their families or losing a parent, and somehow trying to manage with their finances dwindling daily.

Then one day Darrell, the building Super, ran into Jeff sitting on the wall in front of their building staring into space.

"What you up to young man? You're from Iowa right? In 221?"

"Yeah. Jeff. Not doing much of anything. I'm just tryin' to figure out how we're going to make it in this City. We can't really leave either."

"What kind of work you do, or did?" asked Darrell.

"I worked at the Schubert Theatre, with the house crew. We did a little of everything. Any chance for a professional career is pretty well shot now. I probably can't even get my old job back even if this thing ever ends."

"My daughter, Louisa, wanted to get into show business too. Never happened for her though. She has these three great kids and works for a law firm as a paralegal. Hard for her now as she's trying to do her work and keep the kids happy at home. She won't let them come over to visit me as she's afraid I'll get infected. Ha, doesn't she know I have to go into many apartments now. Everyone is home and something's always going wrong. Just yesterday Mrs. Lee's sink got stuck for the third time this month. And then Mr..."

As much as he liked talking to Darrell, Jeff just couldn't focus on the problems of the other tenants.

It didn't take Darrell long to notice he had no audience for his stories.

"Hey, sorry man. You've got your own troubles. You know my granddaughter is always sending me these youtube videos to watch. Some of them are really funny. You should take a look at them, they'll cheer you up. Hey, maybe you could even come up with one yourself with your theater background, and make other people laugh."

When Jeff got back to his apartment he went on the computer and started to search out entertaining videos directed at everyone sheltering at home. Kids, moms, people working from home, singles. There was something for everyone. For the first time in weeks he laughed out loud. He made his roommates watch the videos that night and they, too, laughed long and hard at the antics and cleverness of so many of these short pieces.

So now each day after he and Larry spent some time looking for work, they talked about their zany ideas. Mike was usually too beat to be part of their creative team, but it did make him happy to be part of the performance. Eventually they made videos covering everything from rural boys coming to New York at the wrong time, pandemic dating tips, and even a humorous little play about how aliens were orchestrating the behavior of humans during the pandemic.

Mike showed a couple of the videos to the Director at the Redwood Acres senior home where he worked, and she decided it would be really worthwhile to have the team there to entertain her depressed and locked down residents. So she suggested Mike get his roommates to do a virtual interview with her, for entry level positions, as there was no other way she could safely and regularly bring them into the facility. Several people on her staff had recently left for more lucrative hospital jobs so she had more than her usual number of openings. Within a week both Larry and Jeff were working at Redwood Acres, mostly deep cleaning the facility much of the day. But they also reserved time to entertain the residents, room by room as each person was in a lockdown mode all day long. The trio would stand in the hall with the resident's door open and do their shtick to shrieks of laughter and requests that they don't leave.

"Stay, stay and do another one, please!" could be heard echoing around the facility. Laughter had returned once again to the halls of Redwood Acres.

Jeff thanked Darrell for his great idea, and pretty soon when they all had some time off, at Darrell's request they went around their own building, and from the safety of the hallways they did several more live performances.

In the years after the pandemic ended, the trio continued to entertain residents of senior centers when they could. Mike went on to get his RN degree and lined up a good position in the ICU at Elmhurst Hospital. His dad recovered, but not fully as he foolishly kept smoking! Larry continued to work at the senior facility and was happily helping the residents he had come to love and respect.

As for Jeff? Unfortunately, he lost his mother to the virus and as soon as he could travel again, went home to Iowa to see his family and participate in a memorial service for her. When he returned to New York, he eventually was able to land a fairly decent job at an off-Broadway theater recently reopened.

One corollary to this story. Remember Emmie, the caregiver who worked for that elderly lady in the building and was accused of stealing her money? Well our good friend Darrell introduced Jeff to Emmie. Now they're happily dating, with the full approval of Emmie's two young children. Even Jeff's Dad has come around to the idea of his son and an "undocumented" person as a couple. But Jeff does have to constantly remind him that no human being should ever be called "illegal"!

And, you know, if things work out for these two, Jeff won't have very far to go at all to line up his two very best "Best" men!

# Covid-19 in a Brooklyn Apartment Building

## Ellen and Hannah

Ellen O'Connor and her husband Bob had lived in the same Brooklyn apartment for 20 years, until one day he just moved out. Said he'd met this wonderful woman, Susan, and they'd been seeing each other for most of the past year. He waited until their only child, Amy, started college in the fall of 2019 to break the news to Ellen. Ellen was immobilized for a few moments, berating herself for how clueless she'd been over the last year. How could she not have figured out all those late nights "at work", she wondered. The truth was that she enjoyed her evenings at home alone with Amy and hadn't really missed Bob enough at the time to question him more.

They decided that the announcement of the demise of their marriage could wait until Thanksgiving, when Amy was scheduled to come home from Cornell. Ellen insisted that Susan was to be nowhere in sight when they told Amy. So following a somewhat strained Thanksgiving dinner, Ellen sat silently while Bob muddled through with some complicated explanation. When he got to the part about them still loving Amy even though they didn't love each other anymore, Amy raced out of the room in tears.

In the months that followed that encounter, Ellen got herself a good divorce lawyer and did quite well in the final settlement, since Bob was a fairly successful accountant for one of the smaller firms. She was a little worried about Amy away at school and brooding, but when they saw each other at Christmas Amy seemed to have accepted their newly split family.

At first Ellen thought she wanted nothing to do with the Brooklyn apartment she and Bob had shared for so long. But then she realized it made little sense to move for several reasons. First, it was the only home Amy had ever known and Ellen wanted her to have some semblance of the familiar when she came home. And then Ellen really loved her building. Many of her neighbors had lived there for a long time, as had she, and she had more than just a passing relationship with a few of them. They would share a coffee or a long visit in the laundry room or in someone's apartment. In fact she had gone to the movies or the theater with a couple of women she was most close to during the many times Bob was out of town, or more likely with Susan, as she later realized. She often told Darrell, the building Super, that this was the best maintained building and he was one of the nicest people in New York. And she really meant it!

So to move out of her building now seemed foolish. Besides that, she owned a boutique bridal salon she had run for the last 15 years, which was literally a block away. Though she always had trendy wedding dresses to sell, much of her business came from complicated and elaborate alterations, mostly through word of mouth. Ten years ago, Ellen had hired two talented sisters named Kim and Mai Tran to help her with the alterations side of the business. The sisters had learned their craft years before in their native Vietnam, and were not only highly skilled but lovely to work with.

But then the major tragedy of the century, maybe even the millennium, hit New York City and the world. By mid March 2020, Covid-19 had resulted in all non-essential stores in New York closing down. For Ellen that hit hard as every wedding ceremony got postponed or even canceled. Ellen couldn't believe her bad luck; in the same year she was finalizing her divorce she also had to shutter her business.

Amy returned from Cornell in late March as onsite school was canceled, and promptly announced she was going to Fort Lauderdale with a girl friend for Spring Break. Ellen felt alone in managing her 19-year-old daughter without the united front she and Bob had always maintained when it came to child rearing. But she could do nothing to stop her daughter, and anyway, she argued with herself, it had been announced early in the pandemic that young people seemed to be fairly immune.

Easter was very sad for Ellen. She was alone and sheltering in place, though she did manage to keep in touch with friends and close family, many of whom lived in Chicago. When Amy returned from Florida, they settled into a routine of sorts. Amy continued with her classes online and Ellen sewed, did jigsaw puzzles, read and talked to her friends and family. She insisted Amy find a place to get tested for Covid-19, and luckily she did test negative for the virus, though many other returning students from Florida, and sadly their extended families, were not so lucky. Turned out young adults and children were more vulnerable than had originally been suspected by the authorities.

One Tuesday in April, Ellen decided she had better take a walk over to her shop as she had not checked on it for more than a week, especially since she didn't have boards on the windows to prevent a potential break-in. On this particular morning she was surprised to see someone sleeping on the step of the building, directly in front of the entrance door. Lately in New York, and most other major cities, the homeless problem had become very difficult during the pandemic when city governments were struggling to come up with solutions. Although Mayor De Blasio had requisitioned unused hotel rooms for some of the 80,000 or so homeless in the City, for many reasons the plan was not working.

Now Ellen felt apprehension knowing she would have to first wake up and then confront this homeless person so she could get into her store. She had her mask and gloves on, but wondered if she should look for a police officer as she had no intention of shaking the person awake. As she got closer, she was able to take a better look at the sleeping individual and realized she was looking at a very young girl whose unmasked face was peeking out of her blanket.

"Excuse me," Ellen called out from at least six feet away. "You're in the doorway of my shop and I need you to please get up." Nothing, not even a twitch. Well that makes sense, thought Ellen. If she can sleep through sirens she can certainly sleep through my timid voice!

In the next instance several teenage boys came by and started poking the girl through the blanket with their feet. "Hey, can I get under that blanket with you?" They burst into raucous laughter at their own wit. The girl sat up dazed and looked around, obviously startled by their loud and aggressive behavior.

Although Ellen was not an active advocate for the homeless, she nevertheless felt a sense of outrage that the girl was being treated this way.

"It's okay," she shouted at the boys. "I own the store. I'll take care of this." Now the girl was standing up, folding up her blanket and picking up her backpack. "I'm so sorry, Miss. Sorry. I'll find somewhere else to go. Don't worry. I'm really sorry."

"It's okay," Ellen assured her. "If you have a mask maybe you could come inside for a few minutes. I'm not supposed to let anyone in the store, but you look like you could do with a place to sit down."

"Sorry, Lady, I don't have a mask."

"My name is Ellen and I just happen to have an extra unused one in my purse. You can keep it. It's cloth and not the really good N95…"

Ellen realized she was babbling in the fear that maybe she was doing something very foolish. She handed the girl the mask and waited while she put it on. Maybe this girl was a drug addict or a thief. Though she really didn't seem belligerent or looked like she was strung out, argued Ellen's other "hand".

Finally, Ellen unlocked the store and invited the girl to come in with her.

"What's your name, honey?" asked Ellen.

The girl hesitated, then smiled at a wedding poster on the wall that had a designer named Hannah's signature slanted on its corner.

"It's Hannah," she said. Ok, Ellen thought. So she doesn't want me to know her name. I can live with that. She has her reasons.

"Can I use your bathroom?" the girl calling herself Hannah asked.

"Of course, dear. It's just in the back." And then Ellen wondered if there was anything of value she had left in the back of the store. The coffee pot was near the bathroom so Ellen went back to put it on. Suddenly she heard the sound of loud sobbing coming from the bathroom, and knew she had let herself in for a much bigger problem.

"Honey, is there anything I can do for you? Can I call someone?"

Hannah came out of the bathroom and told her she was okay. She said she had just banged herself on the side of the sink and it hurt.

Ellen wasn't born yesterday and knew there had to be something major going on in this girl's life. Maybe she'll open up a bit if we sit down together, Ellen thought.


"Ok, let's have something to drink. There might even be some creamer in the fridge that hasn't gone sour yet."

Being careful to keep her distance at the table, Ellen wondered how best to find out what *was* going on. Maybe a direct question was the best approach, she thought.

"So, tell me. What's a young girl like you doing sleeping outside? It's not even that warm yet. Did something happen with your family?"

"Your shop is so pretty. I used to pass it by on my way home from school, but now…" the girl deflected. She stopped speaking, afraid that she had already given too much away so she went back to the topic of wedding dresses.

"I love how you dress the mannequins. So pretty. So last night I was just out for a walk and then," --here she gave a silly laugh-- "one minute I was, like, looking at them through the window and the next I was asleep. I should probably go. I'm sure my mom must be looking for me." Though that certainly didn't explain a girl walking around Brooklyn at night with a blanket.

Ellen thought the girl to be about 14, though she was quite small and could have been younger. She had curly black hair cut in a flattering style that reached past her shoulders. She was wearing a worn beige sweater and torn blue jeans that had seen better days.

"Honey," Ellen tried again. "If things are not good for you where you live now maybe someone can help."

That was too much for the girl as she broke down and sobbed into her elbow.

Despite all she had read and heard about the virus, Ellen took a big chance and took the girl into her arms, rocking her as she would a baby.

"Please Honey, can't you tell me what's going on? And is your name really Hannah?"

"Yes it really is. That's why I was looking at your poster. It seemed to be a sign maybe I had come to the right place."

The girl pulled out a tissue from her backpack, moved the mask slightly to rub her eyes, and sighed deeply before starting her story.

"My mom used to work in food service at the high school. But that job went away last month with Covid and things have been really hard for all of us, especially me and my twin brothers. They're 10. So she got a job at a pizza place a few weeks ago. She hands out orders at the door. The trouble is she works every day from 4 to 10 pm. And now she has a new boyfriend who's really creepy and is hanging around our place a lot when she's not there."

Ellen didn't like where this story was going but she encouraged Hannah.

"This guy, his name is Mac, is always touching me when my mom isn't around. I don't like it. Last night he was drinking a lot and swearing and yelling at my brothers. I was trying to get my homework done but then I heard him come to my door even though I put a chair up against the knob. But he pushed hard and the chair fell over. I guess it was good he was really drunk as he fell on the floor, but he dragged me with him. I hit him hard and got away from his awful hands." Her voice caught as she let out a large sob.

"Then I ran out of the room. I don't remember really doing it but I grabbed my backpack and this blanket off the chair before I ran. Ellen, I'm so scared for my brothers, but I knew I was really in trouble so that's why I ran. I have to make sure my brothers are okay. What should I do?"

Ellen knew she was way out of her depth on this one. So she told Hannah they'd have to call the authorities. Her brothers needed to be checked on and some safe arrangements made for Hannah.


Hannah suddenly got a faraway look and then went on to something else.

"I really like one of my teachers, Ms Wilson, and trust her. Like I always tell her things. You know, like what's happening at home. And she always helped me to deal with whatever it was. She's my art and design teacher and, like, she told me I have a lot of talent. But now I don't see her

99

anymore. I hate this virus." She started to cry again but then got ahold of herself and continued with her story.

"We only have one computer and have to share it for school for all three of us. I can't tell my Mom about Mac. She wouldn't believe me even if I told her." Then she brightened as she abruptly switched topics and came up with a new idea.

"How about if I come to work for you, Ellen, and design some new dresses for you? I learn fast. If you call the police, we'll all have to go to foster care. That happened once before and it was terrible. Can I just call my mom to make sure she's home and the boys are okay?"

Ellen agreed and Hannah called her mother, asked about the twins, and told her she couldn't stay in the apartment with Mac there. She said she was safe, implying that social services had put her in a foster home, which of course wouldn't happen without the knowledge of the mother. But Hannah's mother didn't seem too concerned once she knew Hannah was okay, as far as Ellen could make out from the one-sided conversation.

"Okay Mom, I'll be in touch in a few days. Kiss the boys for me and tell them I'll be back soon."

"Hannah, I can't just walk away and leave you on your own," Ellen sighed.

"Maybe I can work for you." Hannah tried again. "I got some great new ideas when I looked at the mannequins last night."

"Listen *I* have an idea, Hannah. Are you up for a bit of a walk to meet some really wonderful friends of mine?"

Ellen had successfully applied for the government's pandemic Payroll Protection Program meant for small businesses, and was able to keep paying her two employees Kim and Mai. In return they took some dresses home with them and continued with the alteration part of the business. So far only two brides had outright canceled their weddings, and several others hadn't set a new date yet. Ellen decided if anyone needed additional alterations later on down the road she wouldn't charge them again. The way people were putting on weight with the gyms closed, she knew further alterations would be extremely likely!

Although Kim and Mai knew no one was supposed to be in their apartment, they put their masks on and were more than happy to show Hannah what they were working on. She was so exuberant about their craft that she asked if she could stay for a while and watch them work. Ellen went outside to the hallway and called Child Protective Services but as expected she got voicemail and could only leave a detailed message. But a social worker did call her back within the hour. This social worker was sympathetic, though she said she had so many cases right now it was very hard to keep up. She explained that the hardest part of her job was finding out about all the *other* people in the lives of her families. With the pandemic it was very difficult to know what was going on in homes in general. She told Ellen that the number of cases of child abuse and domestic violence had increased to alarming levels, especially among poorer families where living space was at a premium and people were packed together for hours at a time.

Ellen decided to take a chance and make her case. She asked the social worker if they could speak with the mother, and then she would like to see about having Hannah temporarily placed in her home. The social worker said she'd make a few calls and be back in touch. In the meantime Ellen asked Hannah if she'd like to stay a night or two in her apartment until things could get things sorted out, and she shouted out, "Yes, and can I please come over here and learn everything I can from these ladies!"

Ellen did eventually meet Hannah's mother who was more than willing to have Hannah stay with Ellen in her apartment if it meant no more scenes with Mac. The twins came over to visit on occasion, and stayed over on the nights when their mother had to work late. After the pandemic was over and Hannah's mother returned to her old job at the school, she eventually threw Mac out as she said he had become a drain on her finances, contributing nothing. Ellen saw bruises on Hannah's mother's arms on more than one occasion and was glad she had come to her senses.

Things have a funny way of turning out, don't they? Hannah was very happy in her new foster home with Ellen, and actually made a wonderful companion for her once Amy returned to school. After Amy got over her initial feelings of jealousy she came to a truce, and even made up with her father, actually spending some of her time with him and Susan.

When the public schools eventually opened in the fall of that year, Hannah started 10th grade. Once again she is a happy student and loves school. Her favorite class is of course Home Economics, though it has a new-fangled name like Domestic Arts that Ellen can never remember. Ellen is paying for Hannah to take a textile design class at the art institute near her apartment. It is obvious to Ellen and the Tran sisters that Hannah has the talent and drive to eventually become an excellent dressmaker and designer.

And now that the pandemic is over, and brides have multiplied exponentially, Hannah spends every Saturday doing her favorite thing of all - helping at the bridal shop.

# Covid-19 in a Brooklyn Apartment Building

## Darrell

Darrell Robinson, the beloved Superintendent of his Brooklyn building, joined his first ever protest march in the late spring of 2020 during the Covid pandemic. For Darrell, a mild mannered and easy going person, this decision was monumental and would leave a lasting mark on anyone who knew him.

Darrell grew up in New Orleans where he met his wife, Erma. A few years after they married, they made the move north to New York for better opportunities. Louisa, their only child, was born and raised in Brooklyn. Darrell began his career in NY at several local Marriott Hotels, eventually becoming supervisor of maintenance services for one of their facilities. And then the owner of the building where he and his family lived asked him if he'd be interested in becoming the Super. When he agreed to this new and much better opportunity, he and his family moved into a first floor apartment rent free.

Darrell always maintained good relations with the residents, mainly because of his can-do attitude and friendly disposition. But unknown to the tenants, or really to anyone other than his immediate family, he carried a heavy burden from his early days in New Orleans. Tragically, in the 1980's Darrell lost his two brothers at different times, but in both cases at the hands of the police. His elder brother, Tyler, died in police custody, but the resulting autopsy indicated only that he had died of heart failure. The family knew Tyler had no history of heart disease. Unfortunately at the time they had little money or influence to hire a good lawyer who might have been able to uncover what had actually happened.

And then a few years later his other brother, Ward, died when he was shot by police during a robbery of a 7-Eleven store. Ward had gone to the store to pick up a package of cigarettes. He was an innocent man caught in the crossfire of someone else's crime. It was after the death of his second brother that Darrell and Erma made the decision to move north and start fresh. When Erma was pregnant with Louisa, Darrell fervently prayed every day of her pregnancy that their child would not be a boy.

Over the years living in New York, Darrell was grateful that his circumstances were good, his daughter attended excellent schools, his wife had a rewarding job in the local library, and he liked most aspects of his job. In truth, though, the tenants never became close friends to the Robinson family, no matter how many years they were neighbors. He was always "Darrell" to them and they were always Mr. or Mrs. So-and-So to him. He didn't mind though. That was the relationship anyone would have had in his position he rationalized.

Some years after the Robinsons moved in, the area they lived in had started to become gentrified and rent prices exploded. The tenants were a diverse lot, though mostly white, and frankly most of them rarely, if ever, gave a thought to what life is like for a black man in America. With his family history, Darrell was always fearful of the police and what they could do to him, innocent or not. It didn't matter where he went or what he did, if he saw a cop anywhere nearby, his tendency was to avoid eye contact and head in a different direction.

When Covid-19 hit and the media was reporting African Americans were being affected and dying in much greater numbers than any other group, Darrell had something new to worry about. Prior to the pandemic, his daughter Louisa and his three beloved grandchildren used to come by the apartment for a visit several times a week. Now talking with his family on Skype was not quite the same. Darrell had always expressed his love in a highly physical way and not being able to do that made him lonely, and even depressed on occasion. None of the neighbors in his building ever knew, though, what was going on behind the friendly face he always showed to his "public".

As the whole world watched, thousands of New Yorkers died of the pandemic during the month of April. In Darrell's building, the elderly Mrs. Levine and the refined Thea Kazan both died of the virus while all the other tenants were affected in one way or another. There were the young men from Iowa who lost their jobs, and health care workers working more hours than they cared to in mortal danger for their lives every day. But there were also some good stories like Ben and Naomi, and Cheryl and Mario who met because of Covid-19. One other good result of the pandemic, Darrell liked to tell anyone who asked was that he had almost no turnover of apartments to worry about!

Memorial Day found Darrell enjoying a quiet evening watching a baseball movie on Netflix. It had been a good day because, for the first time in months, he had spent the afternoon with his daughter and grandchildren in a local park. There they could social distance more safely than in his apartment. He was starting to feel some semblance of normalcy and thought that maybe life could return as it (almost) had been before the pandemic.

But as Memorial Day was winding down, Darrell turned on the 11 o'clock news. That was the moment when life changed again for most of America. All hell had broken loose when a tape was made public, showing a white police officer with his knee on African American George Floyd's neck for nearly 9 minutes, long enough to kill the man. Three other officers were crouched down nearby and did nothing to stop the killing.

Something snapped in Darrell. Before, when he had seen reports of other black men killed by police, he somehow rationalized the incident away or tucked it into a recess of his mind, as he had in the case of his brothers. But now he could no longer control the building rage he was feeling about the injustice of a murder committed by yet another white cop on a black man. Floyd had been accused of passing a fake $20 at a small grocery store in Minneapolis. Could that be all, he wondered, to cause a man to lose his life? There must be more to this story. But no one was saying there was any more, and so when protest marches started up all over the country he knew he could not sit this one out.

That first weekend saw huge demonstrations and looting all over the country which didn't feel okay to Darrell, so he decided he wouldn't participate. But then when the President ordered the military to Washington to clear protestors with tear gas and riot gear just so he could hold a Bible up outside a church for a photo-op, to Darrell that was the last straw.

The day after that incident Louisa called to say she was going on the march in Times Square the next evening and would be bringing the children with her.

"Is that smart, Louisa," asked Darrell, always worrying about safety. "It might not be okay for the kids. And then there's still the virus."

"This is bigger than the virus, Dad. We're making history. The kids need to protest this injustice as much as I do. Maybe things will be better for them if we can change things now. We have to go."

"Okay, then I'm going with you."

"Dad, I'm not comfortable with you joining us. What about your asthma? Didn't you see all that tear gas on TV?"

"I'll be okay with my mask. I'm sure the NYPD is not out to get peaceful protesters."

"Dad, c'mon they're cops. I don't have to tell *you*. Or have you already forgotten about the uncles I never got to meet?"

"No I haven't. And that's why I have to go this time. My parents didn't march in the 60's. I didn't do anything when Rodney King was killed or Trayvon Martin or my own brothers. I didn't protest about all those mass killings in churches and schools, carried out every single time by a *white* man. I never said anything. Well now I'm going to stand up for our rights and every other black person in this country. It's my time now, Louisa. I'm getting old and I need to say something."

"Okay, Dad. But you wear that N95 mask I got you, or you're not coming with us. You hear?"

"Yeah, yeah. Who's the parent here, huh?"

"Okay we'll meet up at your place after I finish work tomorrow. Do you have a safety helmet you could wear? I'm not kidding Dad."

"I'll be fine. But I'm really worried about the kids going."

"There's a bunch of kids going from their school organized by one of the parents, so we'll join up with them. Not sure why they can march together, but not go to class together. That sure would help all us parents trying to do this teaching thing *and* work!"

All that day Darrell had misgivings about the family's participation when he watched the police response throughout the country, even against people doing nothing but marching peaceably. Late in the afternoon, he ran into Ben and Naomi who had moved in together, reminding him he'd have to get Naomi's vacant apartment ready for a new renter soon. Darrell was very fond of both of them and as a die-hard romantic hoped their relationship would work out.

Ben was carrying a large sign proclaiming "I Can't Breathe!"

"Do you plan to protest?" Ben asked Darrell.

"Yes, this evening. My daughter's not happy about it. She's worried about the virus and the police beating me up. But I think it's really important I go. Why are you two going?"

"For exactly the same reason as you, Darrell. For justice. America has got to change. Hey don't forget to register to vote in November."

"Yep, never missed an election yet." In New York, anyway, he added to himself.

"Stay safe, then, Darrell," Naomi added. Hadn't Darrell's own parents always said that to him when he left the house as a young man all those years ago? When will we stop telling people of color to stay safe? And now we're dealing with a triple pandemic, he thought. So many people out of work, others dying from this virus, or getting killed just for being black.

Later that evening Darrell and his family took the subway to Times Square with hundreds of other people holding signs ready to protest. Darrell was a little uncomfortable on the subway, especially when someone behind him began to cough. He had his mask on and had remembered the helmet last minute. He hadn't really wanted to bring it along but he was also not willing to suffer Louisa's wrath either. Just like her mom, he thought with fondness for the love of his life who had died far too early of a particularly virulent form of cancer.

When the family reached the protest, it was already very loud and busy with a few people breaking windows and grabbing anything they could from the stores.

"No," said Darrell. "I just want to march peaceably. Let's take the kids home. I didn't sign up for this."

"It's okay Dad," Louisa assured him. "Look, there are so many people here and most of them *are* marching peacefully. I'm sure we can stay away from the troublemakers."

Darrell's family, and the others from the children's school, headed towards the rear of the crowd so as not to be near the looters. For the first time in his life Darrell proudly held a protest sign saying "Black Lives Matter". Although he did feel a little self conscious being one of the only people around wearing a helmet. What we do to keep our kids from yelling at us, he chuckled to himself.

Not long into their walk, some of the looters came towards them running away from the police with armloads of stolen property. Darrell tried to steer his family to the sidelines, and though they were able to get clear of the fray, Darrell got caught in the mob. A white police officer got very close to Darrell. They locked eyes for the briefest of seconds before the officer pushed Darrell hard as the cop tried to grab one of the looters. But Darrell didn't fall directly to the ground. Instead the back of his head hit a fire hydrant on the way down. The last thing he heard before he lost consciousness was Louisa screaming, "Dad, no not my dad. Please don't let it be my dad!"

He was carried to an ambulance almost immediately by people screaming at the police, "Not again!" and "How many more black men have to die at your hands?" To make matters worse, the ambulance left before Louisa could get close enough so she was unable to find out about his condition or where he was being taken. She feared she had lost her dad seeing him on the ground unmoving and bleeding. The children were screaming "Granddad!!" over and over when they saw him taken away.

And all around her people had been holding up their cell phones to once again record another instance of police brutality. She put her arms around the children who were sobbing uncontrollably. A white policewoman came over to say she knew where he had been taken, and asked Louisa if they could use a ride to the hospital. She nodded her head yes, and the four of them left the protest march for the officer's car nearby. Louisa wondered if Darrell Robinson would now appear on posters all over the country.

But Darrell did not die that night or even the next. Thanks to Louisa's insistence, that helmet had saved his life the doctors told them later. He was to suffer debilitating headaches for the rest of his life, but thankfully he miraculously survived the fall. He stayed in the hospital for nearly a week until he was clearly on the road to recovery. That didn't keep the news media away and for a time he, Louisa and the children became new household names. Letitia, his five year old granddaughter, said she was so scared they were going to shoot her grandpa too. That clip was played around the world on every form of media available.

And when he returned home the kindness of most of the tenants in his building was extraordinary. Ben and Naomi took turns staying with him in his apartment for a few days when Louisa couldn't be there. He received enough cards, flowers, food, gifts, and money, to last him for more than one lifetime. He was completely overwhelmed by the caring of his own tenants as well as people from far and wide.

When Darrell Robinson eventually died many years later, he had made his mark in this world in no small way. He was a kind man, a man loved by his family and the people he interacted with regularly. He loved life and believed in doing right by others. He could have been another statistic, for those who keep track of these kinds of numbers, at the hands of the police. But for the grace of God and the wisdom of his loving daughter, he would not have survived that attack. Above all, he was a good father and grandfather who wanted nothing more than to live his life out in peace.

Only time would tell if his grandchildren will experience a new world free of killing pandemics, free of fear and reprisals, and a world where the color of their skin will make absolutely no difference whatsoever.

# Acknowledgments and Thanks

Much of this book was written while sheltering at home during the Covid-19 pandemic. If one has anything positive to say about the pandemic, it is that those with creative instincts could no longer use the excuse they were too busy to sit down and write or paint or do a myriad of other creative things!

I want to thank both of my book groups for their encouragement and feedback as I sent them each new Covid-19 story throughout those dark months we could not see each other in person. And to the many friends and family who found the other stories hit a mark or made them think of someone who has had special meaning in their lives.

Thank you to Rabbi Sheldon Lewis, a published author in his own right, for his encouragement and helpful advice. And thank you to my neighbor and good friend, Patti Kahn, for taking the time to read the manuscript and suggest edits. A special thanks to Hakodesh Press Publishing House for their assistance and responsiveness throughout the process.

Much appreciation and love to my husband, David, who shared many insightful comments along the way, and was my foremost critic and cheerleader. And to our children and grandchildren who continue to amaze us with their own forms of creativity and accomplishments - and for their good humor despite spending months sheltering in place.